THE SHANGHAI STRIKE

A SOLAR COMMONWEALTH NOVELLA

JOHN LALLIER

JCL PRESS

By John Lallier

SOLAR COMMONWEALTH
The Eridani Incident
The Indus Incursion
The Promethean Challenge
The Korhvallan Agenda
The Draconis Campaign
The Pygmalion Plot
The Comae Gambit

TALES of the SOLAR COMMONWEALTH
The Shanghai Strike
The Centauri Betrayal

For Jane

AUTHOR'S NOTE

The timeframe for this book begins twenty-two years after the events in *The Korhvallan Agenda*.

CHAPTER I

Zhongnanhai, Beijing, PRC
2048APR20 16:03 CST (2048APR20 8:03 UTC)

Despite his advanced age, Wu Zhongxun strode down the corridor with purpose, nodding occasionally to assistants who jumped to attention as the leader of the nation passed by. Each of these underlings remained silent since a quick glance at Wu's face made it clear that the great man was in no mood for minor issues.

Wu barely noticed the images on the wall, representations of great moments in the nation's history. Most of these images portrayed events that followed the Party's ascension to control of the republic, almost one hundred years earlier. And while there were several outlining the nation's rise to power fifty years later, few if any drew on the past twenty years. The twenty-first century was heralded as China's century, just as the previous century belonged to the Americans. But all that changed in 2020; China was robbed of its moment in the sun. And Wu Zhongxun would never forgive those who perpetrated that theft.

Approaching his destination, Wu did not break stride as he approached the door. The guard stationed there quickly threw the door open and then stood back to allow the leader to continue inside.

As the door closed behind him, Wu surveyed the interior. Compared to other meeting rooms in the complex, this one was small, with a 3-meter-long table in the center. At one end of the table a large high-backed chair dominated the area, with shorter chairs down each side. Opposite the large chair, a video monitor nearly as large as the tabletop spread across the wall. The only other person in the room was a military officer who stood at attention as the door flew open.

"Colonel Sun," the president of the People's Republic of China intoned as he moved to the primary chair, gesturing for the man to take the seat on his left.

"Chairman," Sun Qiliang returned as he took the proffered chair. With numerous titles to choose from, Sun always preferred to acknowledge the leader of the country as the Chairman of the Central Military

Commission, rather than as General Secretary of the Party or President of the People's Republic. As chairman, Wu was the supreme leader of the People's Liberation Army. That was his real source of power.

With a nod to the video monitor, Wu prompted, "Where do we stand?"

Sun flipped open his tablet and with a gesture flung an image to the monitor. On the screen, a map of the eastern coast appeared with numerous red arrows winding from a remote location in the west towards the great metropolis of Shanghai. "Personnel began moving into position at 08:00. As planned, the main strike force is traveling in groups of three or less from various surrounding cities to avoid detection. They will assemble at position 'Snake' by 22:00."

Wu grunted approval and nodded. Sun took this as a signal to continue; with a tap of his hand, new blue arrows were added to the map, "At the same time, individual aircraft are moving into positions at four different bases in Anhui, Jiangsu and Zhejiang provinces. These will launch separately to allow the two squadrons to assemble within twenty kilometers of target air space."

Wu's head snapped up at this, "They are untraceable?"

Sun nodded as his hand swept across his tablet; on the monitor, an image of two aircraft replaced the earlier map. One appeared to be a fixed-wing fighter, while the other was a helicopter; both were draped in black. "The Chengdu J-31 fighter and the Harbin Z-27 attack helicopter. Each is the finest in the world for their purpose. Both have been modified to our requirements and none have any markings that would connect them to Department 828. Even the PLAAF roundel has been left off." Anticipating the chairman's next question, "The same is true of the men – no insignia for rank or position, no indication they are in anyway connected to the PLA."

Wu snorted at that, "Until they open their mouths."

Sun shook his head, "Every one of them knows the importance of this mission. None will speak."

Wu remained silent for a pause, staring at Sun. Finally, he nodded, "Very well, Colonel. Let us hope you are correct." Slapping his hand to the table, "You may proceed." With that he stood up (with some effort) and moved to the door, which opened just at his approach.

Sun immediately switched off the monitor to prevent prying eyes from catching a glimpse. Watching the president of China trundle out the door, the colonel waited until the door again closed before turning the monitor back on. Flipping through other images he had prepared for the meeting but never used, he spoke to the now absent leader, "Do not worry, Chairman. We will succeed. Our century can yet be salvaged."

Commonwealth Office, Shanghai, PRC
2048APR20 19:37 CST (2048APR20 11:37 UTC)

"Why do you insist on doing that yourself?" Argenta Quintilius demanded as she entered the bedroom suite. She lowered herself into an armchair with a subtle exhale of breath.

Given how frequently they had this particular discussion, the Regent never broke his pattern as he moved from the wardrobe to the bed, dropping various articles of clothing into the travel bag that had been placed on the edge, as he answered, "Because I like to do this myself. Why is that not reason enough?" He dropped a dark blue jacket on the top of the pile in the bag and finally turned to face her.

Argenta sighed. "Because you're not good at it. Did you forget what happened during that trip to Buenos Aires last month?" she asked, then tilted her head slightly to the right as she provided the answer. "You forgot to pack socks."

The Regent shrugged, "That's a fashion choice. When I was young, that look was quite popular."

"When you were young, fire was a novelty," Quintilius shot back. Despite appearances, she knew she was nearly twenty years younger than the leader of the Solar Commonwealth. While the Regent appeared to be in his early forties, Argenta looked to be about thirty years older because … well because she was. Unlike her partner, the woman was not the beneficiary of the advanced medical procedures that provided the Regent with eternal youth. Like the rest of the humans around her, she aged normally.

The Regent shook his head, "Well, I don't know about fire, but certainly air conditioning was less common. And color TV. That was definitely new at the time."

"None of which explains your obsession with these mundane tasks," Argenta exclaimed with a wave to the travel bag. "You used to let Clarice and Helga do this in the past. Why do you refuse to let Cyril do it now?"

The Regent stopped and turned to face Argenta, the pale blue shirt in his hands dropping to his side, "As you'll recall, I was never all that comfortable with Clarice and Helga. I just let you bully me into letting them do it because it was expected by the Romans. Well, I'm done trying to impress the Romans." He softened slightly, "These days, I'm just looking to impress one Roman."

Argenta tilted her head, "Assuming that Roman is me, you can best achieve your goal by heeding my advice."

"Fine," the Regent declared, tossing the shirt onto the bed next to the bag. "Cyril can do it. But if I can't find anything that I need, he can go right back to Terra Station for reassignment." He mockingly wagged his finger at his consort, "Just remember, this is your doing."

Quintilius moved closer to the Regent, resting her head on his chest as his arms encircled her. "As are most of your better ideas. Despite your natural plebian inclinations, I am determined to make a proper leader of you," she explained, then in a lower voice added, "in the time I have left."

The Regent sighed – *this old topic*, he thought. Looking down, he admonished her, "I don't want to hear that. We still have plenty of time together. Your work here is not done," he smiled a little as he held her tighter. "After all, you wouldn't want it said that you left the Commonwealth with a half-completed leader. You have a responsibility to future generations to make sure I'm not a complete screw up."

"I'm afraid that is a job of two or three lifetimes. Building the pyramids would have been an easier task. At least the stone doesn't argue every little detail," she joked back.

"So, I'm just feisty stone to you?" he asked in faux shock.

Argenta patted his chest with her hand, "Fine marble. From the famed quarries at Carrara. From this I have fashioned a leader for humanity that will last as long as the Republic itself."

The Regent smiled, "Carrara marble, eh? Not from some quarry near Nova Roma?"

Argenta backed away from his grasp and shook her head. "And you call yourself all knowing? You must be aware that the Ssenn did not allow my people to mine or quarry in our lands. When we required stone, they provided it – in any size or quantity we desired. Of course, it was manufactured, in the same way we fabricate food on our space stations or starships." She held her head a little higher. "That may have been acceptable for the Consulate or the Forum Magnum in Nova Roma, but not here. For this, we need real marble, created by nature over eons. And that means going to Greece or Italy."

"Well, you're the expert," the Regent conceded.

"It would be best if you remember that in the future," she replied. "It will make my work much easier. And then we can avoid unnecessary diversions into your questionable concepts."

"Yes, dear," the leader of the Commonwealth agreed. Eyeing the half-filled travel bag still lying on the bed, he asked, "Are you sure you don't want to accompany me to Australia? It's the perfect opportunity to make sure I don't do something stupid down under."

"No thank you," Argenta replied without pause. "One advantage of my advanced years is that I no longer need to visit deserts if I can avoid them."

The Regent shrugged, "It's not a desert. The area around the base is technically a semi-arid scrubland. And it's not like I plan to bivouac out in the countryside. We'd be touring the base facilities. All enclosed and climate-controlled."

"Little boys playing in the desert with their toys," Argenta declared. "I see no need to subject myself to this spectacle. I find I can accomplish far more in a civilized setting," she spread her arms as if to encompass the surrounding city. "Let me know when you intend to visit Sydney or Melbourne and I will adjust my plans."

The Regent smirked, "I thought all Romans loved military camps." He raised an imaginary sword in his right hand, "Join the Legion and see the world!"

Quintilius shook her head slowly from side to side. "Again, you are betrayed by your reliance on popular entertainments to supplement your limited education. True Romans prize order and civilization above all. This obsession with imperial power was the reason for your Republic's collapse. We knew better."

As often happened, the Regent found himself on the losing end of the argument. "It is *not* boys playing with toys," he mumbled to himself. He was the head of the Commonwealth, as Argenta so frequently pointed out. So, with work finally completed on the base in Australia's outback, he was expected to visit the facility and ooh and ahh over the array of forces stationed there. Just as he would do in several years' time when the base in Canada was finished. *It's part of my job*, he thought to himself. *She's constantly reminding me of the need to attend these ceremonies.* He shook his head. *Next, she'll make fun of my starships.*

"I take it that's a definite 'no' to joining me then?" he verbalized.

Argenta's smile was magnanimous. "As I have said many times, you are capable of learning. That is a most definite 'no', as you put it." She stood beside the Regent, taking his right arm and guiding him to the room's exit, "Now, we'll go watch one of your entertainments while Cyril cleans all this up. I suggest something light and comedic."

"Yes, ma'am," the Regent agreed as he allowed her to take the lead.

Zhongshan Regency Hotel, Shanghai, PRC
2048APR21 01:32 CST (2048APR20 17:32 UTC)

It was a cool, crisp night as Ping Youxia stared down from the top floor of the hotel; his reflection superimposed over the image of the building across the plaza far below. The entrance to the park both buildings bordered was closed at this time of night, as were the nearby entrances to the metro station below his building. Still, there were a few people walking briskly by on the plaza, just as a few taxis still plied the roads below, delivering late night arrivals to the hotel's street-level entrance.

But it was the cold black glass building across the plaza that Ping was focused on. A spattering of lights still shown through windows, just as they no doubt did on his tower. But there the similarities ended. Unlike the hotel, indeed unlike most of the towers in this city, the flag that flew from that other building was not the proper *wuxing hongqi*, the five golden stars on a field of red. Instead, a single yellow star adorned a field of black, fluttering above the city. Black – the color of evil and misfortune. In truth, it was the symbol of his nation's misfortune. It didn't matter to Ping that foreign flags flew above the various consulates in the nearby French Concession; that the Stars and Stripes flew above the American consulate and the Union Jack above the British. Those he could accept, since the flag of the PRC flew above consulates and embassies in New York, Washington and London. No, this flag was the exception. This flag was the insult. This flag was the constant reminder to all in this city that China, on the verge of accession to her rightful place as the world's leading nation had been denied its destiny. This was the never-ending offense.

And now he stood, looking down on that atrocity. He grinned, recognizing that he now stood above the top floor of that building, able to look down onto its roof. His only unfulfilled desire would be to be able to see the occupants of that building – to be able to look down on the enemy. *Soon*, he thought. *Very soon.*

After a quick glance at his watch, he swallowed the contents of his glass and deposited it on the nearest table. A silent nod from the barman standing at the now empty bar reminded Ping that he was the last to leave. He chided himself for drawing undue attention to himself; anonymity was demanded in his role. Still, he pushed the concern aside. It would not matter now. Tomorrow was all that mattered. After tomorrow, all China would know his face.

Commonwealth Office, Shanghai, PRC
2048APR21 06:10 CST (2048APR20 22:10 UTC)

The Regent tried to keep the noise to a minimum as he padded around the bedroom, his shoes clutched in his left hand. Bending down, he brushed his lips across Argenta's brow, causing her to mumble and roll over. *Perfect*, he thought, *she can rest.* He stepped out of the room, closing the door slowly to avoid causing any final noise.

Once in the sitting area, he moved briskly to the couch to finally don his shoes. As he finished that, a low voice interrupted his thoughts.

"Good morning, sir," Cyril declared from the open doorway to the dining area. He carried a mug of coffee forward, placing the steaming container on the table to the Regent's left. "Your luggage is already at the landing area. Would you like anything to eat before you depart?"

The Regent looked up to the man as he sipped from the mug. One thing was certain – the man knew how to make coffee. Much better than what the Regent normally found from the beverage dispensers in the rest of the building, or indeed in any of the Commonwealth offices on planet or in orbit. Shaking his head slightly, he replied, "No thank you, Cyril. I'll grab something on the flight down to Australia."

"Of course, sir. I'll advise the stewards," the younger man responded, then turned smartly and returned to the dining area.

Watching him cross the room, the Regent tried to define just what it was about the man that he found off putting. Was it the strangely wrong, almost-British accent? No; over the years, he had worked with any number of men and women from the isle of Norex and never had any difficultly in that area. Perhaps it was his gaunt build and prematurely thinning hair, which made Cyril appear to be much older than he really was? But that also shouldn't be it – every two or three years, the chief of staff came to the Regent to introduce the latest recruit, the latest addition to the residential staff, the newest man or woman who would be charged with seeing to the Regent's personal needs as he managed the affairs of the Commonwealth.

Hell, even the chief of staff changed – when Argenta chose to step back from her duties as Executive Director, the Regent had promoted Agnete Lindfjeld to that critical post. Now, Tanaka Chie was tasked with filling Lindfjeld's shoes as his most trusted adviser. And maybe that was the real answer. The Regent didn't have a problem with Cyril Rochester; he had a problem with change. Because over thirty years, everyone changed. Jiang replaced Gao; Fitzpatrick replaced Jiang; Ramana replaced Bettencourt. The only person who didn't change in this game of musical chairs was the Regent. *I don't go anywhere*, he realized. *I just watch everyone else move around and move on. I am the constant.*

Drawing the mug to his lips, the Regent sputtered as the cooling liquid startled him. Glancing at the band on his wrist, he quickly stood up. *I have got to stop doing that*, he reflected as he returned the mug to the table and straightened his jacket. It would not do to have him show up late for this morning's flight, especially after rising early specifically to avoid just that outcome. So many people worked so hard to make the Commonwealth possible. The least he could do was show up on time.

Grabbing his tablet and stepping out the door to his suite, he found the lift waiting for him. A quick ascent deposited him on the top-most level. He stepped out of the lift just as a Sentry opened the outer door, granting the Regent easy access to the rooftop of the Commonwealth building. Ten meters further, a Commonwealth shuttlecraft sat waiting on the landing pad.

"Welcome aboard, sir," a smiling woman in a bright red uniform announced as he strode through the open doorway.

"Thank you, Sergeant," the Regent answered as he passed the woman and settled into one of the four empty seats on the craft. With Argenta remaining in the residence and Tanaka back at the New York office, he had the whole cabin to himself today. "Please let Lieutenant Akinshina know we can lift off at her discretion."

"Of course, sir," the sergeant replied as she returned to her seat across from the main door and lifted a handset to speak with the pilot.

A moment later the shuttlecraft lifted off the roof of the Commonwealth tower, pivoting gracefully as it rose above the city below. The Regent connected his tablet to the shuttlecraft's internal network and watched as two F-2 *Arrow* fighters took up position on either side of the boxy shuttle. After a brief pause, the trio shot forward, accelerating quickly out of the urban area.

"Regent, Shuttlecraft *Erin* is on course for Terra Base Australia," the voice of the pilot announced from hidden speakers. "ETA, forty minutes."

"Thank you, Lieutenant," the Regent answered to the air as he smiled at the slight Slavic pronunciation of the shuttlecraft's name, reminding him of the face on VADM Fitzpatrick when he announced he wanted his personal shuttlecraft named for her. It was not the face of a woman who felt honored by the action. Nor was she amused when he explained his reasoning – that the shuttlecraft was half the size of the launch he had christened *Catherine*, so he'd simply extracted four letters from the middle of that name to bestow on the smaller vehicle.

"And what do you plan to call your transit pod?" the admiral asked dryly, referring to the smallest of the auxiliary craft in the Regent's Flight and the only one not capable of planetary landing.

"*Cat*," he shot back with a grin, already prepared for her question. "Your question should have been, 'What will you call the next auxiliary when we build something larger than the launch?' That would have been harder."

Fitzpatrick smiled in return, "Not my problem. I have standing orders not to design anything larger until I'm retired. That can be someone else's headache."

The Regent smiled gently as he recalled the scene, then quickly returned to the here and now. He'd been doing a lot of that recently – recalling moments from months or years earlier as if those events were more recent. Maybe this was normal, he wondered. Not that there was anything normal about his life. *I'm an old man who doesn't age*, he smirked, *with a mind that wanders but forgets nothing. Who do I compare notes with? Who do I go to for advice?*

He leaned back in his chair and closed his eyes. Forty minutes. Not really time to relax. But maybe a few days in the desert would be do him some good. *A few days away from the office, with no crisis demanding my attention.* That was what he needed. *Yes.*

CHAPTER 2

Zhongshan Park, Shanghai, PRC
2048APR21 06:25 CST (2048APR20 22:25 UTC)

Recognizing the sound, Chu Daxia looked up in time to see shuttlecraft *Erin* lift off gracefully from the rooftop landing pad. As the officer in charge of the local Solar Guard Sentry platoon, she was already apprised of the Regent's schedule and the fact that he would be taking the shuttlecraft rather than the larger launch. The launch was too large to land on the tower's roof; when it was used, a clearing in the park directly behind the Commonwealth building served as the designated landing zone. And that meant that the Sentries under her command would have been deployed to secure the area well in advance. Thanks to the Regent's choice of the shuttlecraft for his travel, Chu was spared that assignment, which was why she was able to slip out of the barracks and enjoy an early morning jog through the park instead.

As was her routine when exercising outside the Commonwealth compound, she avoided wearing anything that would mark her as a soldier to the local populace. Instead, she wore a simple t-shirt emblazoned with the name and likenesses of a popular Korean band, plus shorts and running shoes she had purchased from one of the stalls in the shopping plaza adjoining the nearby metro station.

All this was done to allow her to pass for a local and avoid inquisitive stares. And it worked for the most part … at least as long as she kept her mouth shut. Because the moment she uttered more than three words, the shop keepers and others she dealt with recognized that she was not a compatriot from some remote village in China, but an off-worlder. With that revelation, their eyes immediately turned cold and suspicious, and any friendly banter halted in mid-sentence. Coming back to the land of her ancestors turned out to be very different from what Chu had expected so many months earlier.

The fact was, she envied the Romans, Norams and other westerners from her world who served alongside her in the Commonwealth building; they never faced this. The people of Shanghai never questioned their accents, never treated them any differently from the numerous Americans and Europeans who milled about the city. No. That was reserved for her and the few other Han in the compound. Despite appearances, they were outsiders in this land, and the locals never missed an opportunity to remind them of that fact.

Still, it was a beautiful spring day and Chu was determined to enjoy this chance to relax with an invigorating run before she settled into the routine of the day. With the Regent away, it promised to be a quiet, uneventful few days.

Zhongshan Park Metro Station, Shanghai, PRC
2048APR21 06:27 CST (2048APR20 22:27 UTC)

Ping walked nimbly between the food stalls in the lower-level market, and despite the heavy duffle bag he carried, he easily dodged shoppers and fellow travelers as he approached the entrance to the metro station. With a quick glance, he turned to his left and was absorbed by the stream of people moving towards the gates to the trains. The nearby McDonald's was doing a brisk morning business as he kept to the left to avoid the actual queue for the metro ticket gates, instead continuing down to the long row of shops. Entering the second to last shop, he was greeted by a familiar face wearing an unfamiliar outfit, a type of floral smock so often worn by shopkeepers throughout the city.

The woman nodded silently at his approach, then glanced about to insure they were alone in the shop. With a step, she waved Ping through to the back of the shop, then quickly stepped back into place to block access as a curtain closed behind him.

He found a second, similarly dressed woman in the back. Unlike the first woman, this one carried a Type 42 pistol, which she aimed directly at the newcomer. After a brief pause, she nodded and lowered the gun, allowing Ping to continue through a steel door to the next chamber. As he closed that last door, a voice called out, "Welcome, Major."

"Thank you, Captain," Ping replied as his eyes took in the new environs. Behind Captain Xu, several men (and a handful of women) stood ready, all dressed in black uniforms. None bore rank or unit insignia, but nonetheless Ping knew every face. These were the Black

Tigers – his men, each individually selected from various units across the People's Liberation Army years earlier for this precise mission. And after months of training and rehearsal, the time had finally come.

Xu pointed to his left, where a small alcove had been cordoned off by a curtain, "You can change in there, sir."

Ping nodded as he proceeded through the curtain, dropping his duffel bag on the bench inside. Unzipping the top, he drew out his own uniform as well as the Type 42 pistol and Type 44 assault rifle and a flat black rectangle in hardened plastic, a sort of ruggedized mobile phone. This was the critical piece carried by each of his men. The latest in secure, encrypted communications that he was promised was years ahead of anything available to other military forces across the planet. He just hoped it was better than anything used *beyond* the planet.

Stripping off his jacket, he changed quickly.

Jing'An Temple District, Shanghai, PRC
2048APR21 06:55 CST (2048APR20 22:55 UTC)

Albrecht Hirsch sat reading the English-language version of the People's Daily on the tabletop as he enjoyed his morning coffee. Despite being stationed here for the past four years, he had never mastered Chinese and relied on a handful of practiced phrases when the situation required. Not something LCDR Hirsch should be proud of, but then he was off duty and currently out of uniform, so who would notice. Like Chu, Albrecht preferred to travel the city in civilian attire to avoid any undue attention. And as a man of habits, he ventured out each Tuesday and Thursday morning to partake in the local cuisine, as it were. The coffee and danish were not up to the standards of the café he frequented while stationed at the Frankfurt office, but it was still a sight better than the manufactured food products available in the Commonwealth office commissary. It wasn't that the ersatz food was inedible – it was just that it was uniformly bland. Holding up his coffee container, he eyed the corporate logo on the side. *Now this is real coffee*, he considered, made from real beans. Just like at home.

So engrossed was Hirsch with his morning repast, that he failed to notice the two uniformed policemen standing near the street just outside the café. The officers alternated surreptitious glances in Hirsch's direction while carrying on their private conversation.

Hirsch was pulled out of his reverie when the band on his wrist began to vibrate. *Time to go,* he realized as he downed the last of his coffee and rose from the table just as an article on the upcoming Olympic Games flashed into view on the tabletop display. He always used the café's system to read the news since he never brought his own tablet on these outings; there were strict regulations against removing secure, service equipment from the office and as the Solar Base commanding officer, he was expected to set an example. Instead, he settled his tab with a quick tap on the screen of his mobile phone; the locally sourced device was issued to each member of office staff to allow them to pay for services and access transportation while outside the office. It was the only device (other than his band) that he was permitted to take outside the Commonwealth tower.

Stepping outside, Albrecht considered his options. He'd strolled down Yuyuan Road earlier in the morning to visit the café, but given the time, it would be better to take the metro. After all, it was only two stops on the number 2 line. That would leave him plenty of time to change into his uniform and begin his day by 08:00. He turned to his right and headed towards the bright red SM logo over the nearest metro entrance when he finally noticed the two policemen. What made them stand out was their uniforms – not the usual blue of the local constabulary, but the dark olive green of the People's Armed Police. That and the sidearms each carried on his hip. It was also clear that they intended to intercept Hirsch before he could reach the metro entrance.

When the two police were within four meters, one of them called out, "Commander Hirsch." It was a statement, not a question, and the policeman enforced this point as his right hand came to rest on his still holstered weapon. "We must speak with you," he added in conveniently excellent English.

So much for travelling incognito, Hirsch thought, *or trying to feign ignorance of the local language.* Instead, he slowly moved his hands outward from his body. Out of uniform and unarmed, he had no desire to alarm either of these two gentlemen into taking rash action. "I'm sorry. Do I know you?"

"No, Commander. But we recognize you," his partner responded, looking just as ready as the first to take action if needed. "You will accompany us."

"Why?" Hirsch shot back, not accustomed to being detained by the local police.

The first policeman (a corporal Hirsch noted from the shoulder boards) took charge. "Our captain wishes to discuss a matter of some import with you. He was most insistent." The corporal gestured towards the street just as a military vehicle came to an abrupt stop and a rear door opened.

Hirsch drew himself up to his full height of 182 cm; unfortunately, that did not give him any advantage over the two policemen. "This is unacceptable. I am an officer of the Solar Commonwealth," he blustered.

The corporal nodded slightly. "We understand that Commander, despite the lack of uniform." He tilted his head towards his colleague, "Like you, we are soldiers. As soldiers, we are required to obey the orders of our superiors. As a fellow soldier, I hope you can understand our position and accommodate us in this matter." He extended his arm to invite Hirsch to enter the vehicle.

Seeing no alternative, Albrecht decided to play along … for now. "Very well," he declared as he bent his head to enter the car.

"Before you do, would you mind surrendering your mobile device? And your watch?" the corporal asked, extending a hand in anticipation of receiving said objects. "Standard procedure, you understand."

Hirsch understood all too well. "Of course," he replied, removing his wristband and placing it in the waiting hand, before reaching into the inside jacket pocket to retrieve his phone. With practiced skill, he pressed three control surfaces simultaneously with his hand before pulling the device out, activating a feature that was most decidedly not standard issue from the manufacturer. With no evidence of this action visible on the phone's screen, he handed the device to the corporal before entering the rear of the vehicle.

The corporal followed him in, while his partner sprinted around to the opposite side to enter. After closing the door, the policeman opened a small box positioned between the two rear-facing jump seats and placed Hirsch's mobile phone and band safely within. There was an audible click as the lid on the box closed.

Probably some kind of Faraday cage, the commander thought. *I'm really off the grid now!* He felt himself pushed back gently into the seat as the vehicle accelerated into traffic, no doubt making used of its flashing lights and priority lanes to avoid any delays. Despite the completely blacked out windows, he recognized when the vehicle ascended onto the elevated highway that wound through this section of the city.

"Where are we going?" he asked casually.

The expression on the corporal's face remained neutral, "As I indicated earlier, my captain wishes to speak with you. We should arrive shortly."

Something's up, Hirsch decided. *I just wish I knew what exactly.*

Shanghai Metro Line 2, Shanghai, PRC
2048APR21 06:58 CST (2048APR20 22:58 UTC)

Major Ping stood in the access tunnel as the west-bound train passed. Once it disappeared, he checked his watch, then turned to Captain Xu, "Go!"

One by one, soldiers surged forward, jumping down onto the tracks and proceeding west in a sharp, unwavering line. With the limited light available in the tunnel, each man had a light mounted on the side of his helmet; fortunately, the metro in Shanghai did not make use of an electrified rail, relying instead on overhead wires to provide power to each train. Not that the danger of a third rail would have prevented this operation; it would be merely another obstacle to be overcome.

As the group moved down the track, the only other potential threat disappeared as the intermittent lights that spanned the tunnel all went dark. "On schedule," Ping announced, reassuring his troops that they need not fear that an errant train would come screaming down on them from the Jiangsu Road station. With that confirmed, the troops picked up the pace.

One minute later, Ping approached a service door and stopped. Banging on the door with the butt of his pistol, the major stepped back as the door screeched open to reveal more of his troops already in position. Inside, Lieutenant Ma nodded to his superior and beckoned him to enter.

"Sir, we are ready to breach," Ma reported as he led Ping beyond the original service room and into a crudely dug extension that ended at a bare concrete wall. Around him, a group of twelve combat engineers, now caked in dirt and mud, stood at attention. This vanguard team had been active for the past five days, silently digging through meters of earth to give his troops the means to approach the target. Now, only one step remained.

"Well done, Lieutenant. Are the charges ready?" Ping inquired.

"Yes," Ma barked, then held the remote detonator out to Ping.

Taking the device, Ping ordered, "Move your men out to the main tunnel. I will join you shortly." As the men around him complied, Ping stared at the concrete wall and the circular object that had been attached. A ring nearly two meters in diameter was held in place by external bracing. At 20 cm intervals, a red telltale light on a rectangular block indicated the object's status. Once those lights turned green, it was time to leave.

So close, Ping reflected with a grin. He could imagine what lay beyond that wall, but in truth he could not be certain. After all those months rehearsing this moment in the hidden facility in the hills of Guangxi, repeatedly storming a replica that the intelligence experts insisted was exact to the last details, Ping was not so certain. And that was a good thing – it was better to expect problems than to assume all will go as predicted. Now, the time had finally come to find out just how accurate the experts were.

Walking to the end of the newly dug tunnel, the major pressed a single control on the detonator. Immediately, all the red lights on the breaching device turned green; the system was armed. Ping proceeded briskly to the steel service door, and once he was on the other side nodded to the two men who shouldered it closed with another screech of metal. Satisfied, he called out to the group, "Goggles on. Masks on."

Like every other member of his team, Ping pulled down the goggles attached to his helmet and then pulled the breathing mask out of the package attached to his belt. Once he was satisfied that the two items covered his face appropriately, he raised his right arm. Looking around, he waited until all those in view did the same.

"Fire!" he called out as he triggered the detonator. Unlike the expected explosion or muffled whomp that standard breaching charges would deliver, this detonator triggered a blinding light that stretched out for nearly ninety seconds, accompanied by an acrid smell that permeated even through the breathing apparatus. This demolition charge did not blow a hole in the wall through brute force; instead, it combined chemicals and enormous output of energy to burn through 60 cm of concrete, steel and who could tell what else. As the blinding light finally faded, Ping was rewarded with the satisfying sound of a crash as the severed section of wall gave way to gravity and collapsed.

It took five men with pry bars to reopen the steel door after it was warped by the side-effects of the breaching charge. Once the opening was clear, Ping pumped his arm in the air and shouted a muffled, "Go!" On that signal, the first wave of soldiers surged forward.

Commonwealth Office (level 14), Shanghai, PRC
2048APR21 07:02 CST (2048APR20 23:02 UTC)

ENS Monica Barzini entered the operations office on the fourteenth level and approached the duty officer, "Lieutenant, do you know where the commander is?"

LTJG Jonathan Hale looked up from the report he was reading and checked the time on the display. "Still an hour before he's supposed to relieve me," he answered. "Did you check the commissary?"

"If this is Tuesday, it must be Starbucks," the petty officer at the communications console joked.

"Thank you, Peraza. Just don't let Commander Hirsch hear you say that," the lieutenant advised, then look up at Barzini. "There you have it. He's probably on his way back from Jing'An Temple."

Barzini shook her head, "That's just it. We know he was outside – we received a security alert from his mobile a minute ago. But when we tried to locate him, the system could not access his phone."

This caused Hale to sit up and take notice. "Peraza," he called out.

"Already on it," the petty officer replied. "Confirmed. Security alert received at 06:58:13 local time. Location … Jing'An Temple District, near Nanjing Road. Signal lost at 06:59:08." Peraza tapped out more instructions on his display, then looked up in confusion. "Lieutenant? We have a problem. I'm not getting any data from external systems."

Hale reached forward and tried himself, tapping on icons and receiving no connection; he then grabbed the receiver from the telephone on his desk and punched in several numbers before dropping the handset back in its cradle. "You're right, we have no voice or data connections to the local networks."

Barzini was bent over an unoccupied station, peering at the display when she announced, "Sir? Check out the buildings across the street. None of them have any lights on." Flicking through a few more images, she added, "And where's the traffic? Changning Road should be jammed at this time of the morning. There's nothing out there."

Hale brought up the images Barzini was viewing on his own display, then considered the implications. A failure of the local power grid would explain the loss of telephone and internet connections; the Commonwealth building relied on its own internal power, but there was nothing they could do if the city's infrastructure suddenly stopped working.

"Lieutenant, I just lost all external connections," the communications petty officer declared.

"Yes, yes. I know, Peraza. The internet and phone lines are down," Hale returned with a wave of his hand, dismissing an update he already knew.

"No, sir. I mean *all* of our connections are down," Peraza corrected him. "We just lost our link to the Commonwealth satellite network. And I'm unable to raise Terra Station or East Asia Monitor on any channel."

"What?" Hale demanded, jumping to his feet. He stood over the petty officer as he argued, "That's impossible. Our comms connections have no dependence on local power; how could they affect that?"

PO Peraza shook his head, "I don't know, sir. I'm just reporting our status." He made a point of repeating his checks as Hale looked on. "There is nothing wrong on our end, but nothing will connect. None of the standard channels show any activity; even the emergency channels aren't working." He leaned back in his chair and look up at the officer, "It's like someone dropped a lead blanket over all of the antennas on the roof."

Hale straightened up, thinking out loud, "Or like someone is deliberately jamming our systems." His voice trailed off as he considered this, then dismissed it. "But how? Who has that capability?" Any further thoughts on this question were interrupted by an odd rumble, followed by vibration as if a minor tremor was adding to their woes. Then alarms sounded across multiple consoles, with lights flashing for attention.

"Dio mio!" Barzini exclaimed in her native language before remembering the others in the room. "Are we under attack?"

CHAPTER 3

Commonwealth Office (level 14), Shanghai, PRC
2048APR21 07:04 CST (2048APR20 23:04 UTC)

"I don't know," LTJG Hale nearly shouted, spinning around as if distracted by all the flashing warnings. Frustrated, he ordered, "Peraza! Turn off that damned racket in here. We all know something's wrong. I don't need all that to tell me."

"Yes, sir," the communications chief returned and after a moment, the hooting alarms stopped … at least in the operations room.

The operations officer exhaled sharply, relieved to be able to think clearly again. "Ensign, where is the problem? I need to know what's happening."

Barzini's hands flew over the display in front of her, swiping and stabbing at various controls. "Atmosphere breach. Lower levels; trying to localize." A few more gestures on the console's surfaces yielded results, "Sub-level three; one of the storage rooms. A massive spike in thermal energy a moment ago. The system has locked down the area to isolate the problem."

Hale was even more confused than before, and his expression showed that. "What? How?" he began.

Barzini threw up her hands, "I don't know, sir. According to the manifest, nothing in that room is supposed to be flammable or hazardous."

Hale rubbed at his temples, then reached his decision. "Ensign, get some of your people down there. I need answers."

"No!" a new voice shouted from the open doorway. All heads turned to spot the source. In the doorway stood a sizeable woman with a shock of short red hair, her green uniform in sharp contrast to the blue attire of the group in the operations room. "We're in lockdown!"

Hale grew frustrated, "Stand down, Sergeant. We're handling this."

"No, sir. Base security can handle internal issues, but the Guard handles external threats," SSGT Heather Mackenzie countered as she entered the room. Before Hale could argue that point, she raised a single finger on her right hand, while cupping her ear with the left. "Wait one," she instructed the Base officer while she turned her attention to an unseen person, "Leekpai? Who's in the ready room?" She paused, presumably receiving the answer from CPL Leekpai in the Sentry CIC on level twelve. "OK. Send Niandu and Ali down to sub-level three. I've locked out the lifts below level five, so they'll have to take the stairs. Control access at each level; I don't want to lose containment." She paused again before adding, "OK. And I want the platoon in full armor in ten. No exceptions." With that, Mackenzie dropped her hands to her side and turned to Barzini, "Ensign, I need your people to move everyone above level five. Now."

Hale blew. "What a minute, Sergeant! Where's Captain Bruttius?" he demanded.

The sergeant turned to face the senior officer present, but retained her take-charge attitude, "Captain Bruttius is with the rest of Fourth Platoon, Lieutenant. In Australia, awaiting the Regent."

Hale blinked, silently chiding himself for forgetting that detail. The Solar Guard Sentry force was stationed here because of the Regent's residence on the upper levels. Since he was away, half of their force had travelled with him. Still, that didn't put Mackenzie in charge. "Then where is your platoon leader, Lieutenant Chu?"

Mackenzie hitched her thumb over her shoulder, "Out there. Just like Commander Hirsch." The Guard sergeant saw no reason to pull punches now; not with a lowly JG questioning her authority. "That makes me the senior Sentry on site, which makes this situation my responsibility. Per regulations."

Hale wasn't backing down either, "Sergeant, we don't know that this is an external threat. It's also possible that an explosion in the lower levels is in some way connected to whatever caused the city's power failure."

Mackenzie shook her head in disgust, "Impossible. A gas leak or transformer overload wouldn't breach our walls. An IAD wouldn't breach our walls. One of the local's warheads couldn't!" She pointed to Barzini, "And as your own security officer can tell you, there's nothing on sub-level three that could do it either. So, if it happened, it's definitely an attack."

The operations officer sighed; this was all more than he could explain. *Maybe Mackenzie is right*, he considered, as much as that thought made him sick. He turned to his security officer, "Ensign Barzini, Sergeant Mackenzie is in charge. Assist her people in any way she requires."

"Yes, sir," Barzini replied. "I'll get that evacuation going," she added as she began giving instructions to the security team.

"Lieutenant, you are still in command of the base," Mackenzie corrected. "I am only taking charge of our defense."

Hale nodded. "Understood, Sergeant. But to be accurate, this is an office, not a base."

Mackenzie shook her head. "No, sir. Right now, we are a base under siege, with key personnel already missing in action. We need to get control of the situation before anything else goes wrong."

Commonwealth Office (sub-level 3), Shanghai, PRC
2048APR21 07:05 CST (2048APR20 23:05 UTC)

Ping's forces quickly spread out into the chamber, pushing aside various containers as well as several racks of shelving that had been damaged by the collapsed section of wall. All were surprised to find the room fully illuminated.

Four soldiers moved to the room's only door on the far wall, with three taking up firing positions while the fourth stood ready to jam a pry bar into the door frame to force an opening. With a nod from the senior rifleman, the man with the pry bar threw his full weight into the act … but with no results. After several attempts to find a seam he could exploit, he turned to his leader for instructions.

Captain Xu looked on. The team brought hydraulic tools in addition to the pry bars, but those still required the operator to find some crack in the surface to exploit. Instead, Xu ordered, "Charges!" An engineer rushed forward to place an explosive device on the resisting portal. Once it was affixed to the door, he stepped back and gestured for the fire team to do the same, the group using the remaining rows of shelves for cover. With a nod from Xu, the engineer set off the charge with a loud womp.

Rushing forward, the engineer quickly inspected his handiwork before turning back to Xu and shaking his head.

Ping watched all this while standing next to the original breach. *Incredible!* he thought. *Ten meters into the assault, and already the experts are proven wrong!* They'd been told to expect the type of steel-clad doors you would find in the basement levels of any office tower across the country. Instead, the aliens replaced these with more of their high-tech wizardry. *But why? This is a simple storage room; why are they protecting it as if it were a vault with precious artifacts?*

In the end, it really didn't matter why. Ping's orders were quite clear – move at speed to secure the building. There was no turning back at the first obstacle. Thumbing the control on his radio, he instructed, "Lieutenant Ma. Bring up the torches; we need to cut our way out." He released the button and moved to find a crate to sit on; this was going to add considerably to the original schedule.

Terra Base Australia, Queensland, Australia
2048APR21 09:05 AEST (2048APR20 23:05 UTC)

Under FLT Akinshina's expert touch, *Erin* glided softly out of the bright morning sky and settled onto the tarmac at Terra Base Australia. After a brief pause to shut down the drive system, SGT Amani opened the left-side hatch and stepped down to stand beside the craft. Seconds later the Regent stepped out, smiling and nodding to the assembled crowd.

Per the Regent's standing orders, no band was present and no recorded music was played. The leader of the Commonwealth held very definite opinions about such pomp when directed at himself. It was fine if the defense services wanted to have anthems and martial music played at their ceremonies, but all that ended if they sought in any way to honor him.

A small group of officers stood waiting a dozen meters from the shuttlecraft, with an honor guard bearing various flags assembled behind them. As those flags fluttered in the surprisingly cool breeze, three of the officers stepped forward and stopped two meters from the Regent, allowing him to close the gap at his leisure.

In the center was the base commander, CDRE Rahma Hamed. To her right, BRIG Kang Jin-Ho of the Solar Guard First Ranger Brigade stood several centimeters taller than the others. GCAP Frida Eiriksdatter of Solar Flight's First Fighter Group standing on Hamed's left completed the trio of representatives for the three services assigned to the base.

As the officer charged with command of the facility, Hamed acted as spokesperson. "Regent, on behalf of my colleagues and all of the personnel assigned, welcome to Terra Base Australia," she announced.

"Thank you, Commodore Hamed. After all these years, it is a pleasure to see what you've built here," the Regent replied, exchanging a hearty handshake with Hamed, then turning to Kang and Eiriksdatter while adding "Brigadier" and "Captain" at the appropriate moment.

With introductions completed, the commodore took the lead, ushering the Regent away from the shuttle. "If you'll come this way, sir," she instructed as she led the group to a waiting vehicle. From the pale blue shading of the machine's exterior, it appeared that this particular conveyance was assigned to the local Solar Base personnel. Inside, the Regent noted that the temperature was at least four degrees cooler than even the early morning outside temperature. "We'll begin at the base operations center," Hamed explained.

The Regent nodded idly, commenting, "Excellent," as he settled into his chair. *It is going to be a long day.*

Commonwealth Office (sub-level 2), Shanghai, PRC
2048APR21 07:07 CST (2048APR20 23:07 UTC)

Two bulky figures trundled down the stairwell single file; dressed in their combat armor, it was impossible for the Sentries to stand side-by-side. Which was just as well – standard protocol called for the second man (or woman in this case) to cover the soldier on point from any threats from behind.

PVT1 Felix Niandu came to a halt on the stairwell landing. With an open channel to CPL Leekpai in the CIC, he called out, "In position. Release security door B-nine-two-nine."

After a brief pause, the corporal responded, "Released."

With a nod to his partner, Niandu pressed a gauntleted hand to a control and the security door slid into its recess. Following the same procedure they used at each previous level, he brought his weapon up quickly in expectation. Once again, there was no one on the other side. Another nod to Ali and he passed through the open doorway.

PVT2 Mahira Ali followed, then announced, "Through. Seal access door B-nine-two-nine." The heavy door slid back into place, locking with a heavy thud. "Proceeding to sub level three," she informed their controller.

The Sentries continued down the next set of stairs, the heavy boots of their armored suits echoing in the confined space. Reaching the bottom and the final security door, Niandu looked at Ali, "This is it." With a flick of his eyes to the heads-up display built into his helmet's faceplate, he polarized the transparent section of the helmet, turning it into a dark grey mirror. Ali followed suit, a necessary precaution in case someone on the other side decided to employ flash-bangs against any defenders.

"Release security door B-nine-three-zero," the senior private requested, checking the charge level on his Type 3 pulse gun.

"Released," Leekpai answered.

With an audible exhale, the larger Sentry ordered, "You go low." He didn't wait for a response as he pressed the control. Even before the door fully retracted, he pushed through with his weapon at eye level.

Ali followed, aiming from her crouched position; both panned across the open hallway, searching for targets. "Clear," she announced.

"Clear," Niandu confirmed, then instructed her to, "Take point." Even in their armor, Felix stood 11 cm taller than Mahira. In tail position, he had no difficulty seeing past her, but if they were reversed, she would see little but his back. "Control, corridor appears clear. Where are our targets?" he asked Leekpai.

The familiar voice replied, "Thermal readings clustered in southeast corner. High thermal readings."

Niandu nodded involuntarily, a gesture neither Leekpai nor Ali could see. "Moving now," he said, both to update the corporal as well as a prompt to his partner.

The pair moved cautiously, halting at each sealed door along the way to confirm that nothing was amiss. As they moved forward, they noted a hissing sound with occasional pops – something definitely out of place on a sub-level used mostly as long-term storage. Finally, they reached the end of the corridor, where it formed a T with the connecting corridor.

Staying just out of the cross-passage, Ali eased her weapon passed the corner, using the sight camera to reveal any obstacles to come.

The image on her heads-up (mirrored on Niandu's so that both knew what they were heading into) was filled with a flash of blue-white light. The targeting computer quickly compensated, allowing them to clearly make out a steady stream of intense heat cutting through a door already marred by scorch marks.

"Control, we have a problem," Niandu informed his superior. "Whoever it is, they're trying to cut their way out of Storage Room B-three-zero-five." He waited a few seconds to see if this would draw a response; with none forthcoming, he prompted, "Orders?"

Before the corporal could answer, the cutting abruptly ceased and with a mighty clang, the severed door fell into the corridor. At once, bodies began to spill through the opening and one of the figures in black must have spotted Ali's outstretched gun. One shot was quickly followed by several more as bullets flew down the corridor.

By instinct, PTV2 Ali fired from her prone position while Niandu edged into the corridor just enough to give himself a clear line of fire. Bolts of energy from their pulse guns quickly cut down several of the intruders as they surged from the now open doorway, but more were coming up fast behind them. The replacements were arriving faster than the two Sentries could halt their partners. At the same time, a steady drum of fire from the horde was chewing up the walls of the corridor and now thudding against the Sentries' exposed armor.

Niandu reached a decision. "Fall back!" he shouted, desperate to ensure he was heard over the din of battle. He tapped Ali's helmet to make certain she got the message, then the two of them dashed back up the corridor. "Control! Open door nine-three-zero!"

"Wait one," was the response they received.

"Now, Control!" he shouted back, not willing to debate the issue. They were halfway up the corridor when they both felt thuds against their armor. As one, they turned about, continuing to back-pedal up the corridor as they kept their eyes focused on the mob in black closing behind them. Bolts from their guns again cut down the forward figures, but the bullets continued unabated thanks to the ever-growing force behind them.

"Screw this," Niandu muttered and thumbed his weapon to its higher setting. Now a steady beam of energy cut through their opponents like a scythe as Ali continued to pick off individuals with single bolts. "Control!" Niandu shouted again.

"Open," Leekpai confirmed, just as Niandu's partner let out a scream.

Niandu looked down to see Ali slowing, still firing one handed as her left hand grabbed at her leg. Still swinging his own fire left and right, Niandu slowed and stared down to see a metal rod inexplicably protruding from the private's left thigh, small fractures in the green armor around the rod indicating it had somehow penetrated what until that minute Niandu had believed was their impervious protection.

Ali was now dragging the damaged leg, hopping backwards with her one steady appendage. "Go," she called back, not letting her fusillade wane. "Leave me."

"No!" Niandu countered as he grabbed her under the left arm, pulling her up while glancing back. The open doorway was only five meters away. Bullets continued to ping off his armored body, when he was startled by a sudden starring of the transparent face shield. Somehow, one of the bullets had created a minor fracture in the material. His eyes were quickly pulled from this unexpected turn when a second metal rod suddenly appeared embedded in the wall, centimeters from where his helmet had been a moment earlier.

With urgent need he leapt the final meter through stairwell doorway, tossing Ali onto the lowest tread as he slammed the control to close the portal. He caught a fleeting glance of their pursuers less than twenty meters down the hall as the door slid into place. "Control, seal nine-three-zero!" he demanded and rushed to check on his partner's vitals. Their armored suits were designed to provide limited first aid, but Niandu could see a red mixture bubbling from the small fissures in the broken armor around the rod. "Send reinforcements. And a medic."

"Private Niandu, what is your situation?" a new voice demanded; SSGT Mackenzie, he realized.

Niandu let out a heavy breath, finally noticing the sweat dripping down his face despite the environmental controls built into his suit. "There are a hundred or more. Special forces. We took out maybe twenty … maybe less. They control the level now." He paused as the steady drum of automatic weapons fire abruptly stopped; it was replaced by heavy thuds as if the enemy were trying to batter the door down. *They'll bring up their cutting tools next*, he realized. "They have the means to cut through the security doors, so we can slow them down but not stop them." He glanced down at the rod protruding from Ali's leg. "And they have some kind of weapon that can punch through our armor. Ali needs evac."

"On their way, Private," Mackenzie responded. "I just need you to hold on for another minute."

An exhausted Niandu looked up the stairwell in anticipation, then returned his attention to the door. Raising his weapon, he answered, "OK, Sergeant. Another minute."

CHAPTER 4

Commonwealth Office (sub-level 3), Shanghai, PRC
2048APR21 07:19 CST (2048APR20 23:19 UTC)

Major Ping walked down the corridor confidently, moving from side to side to get around medics tending to the wounded and fallen bodies that would never again rise of their own accord. Casualties ran high for this first encounter with the alien super-soldiers, but still the senior officer was pleased. Despite nine dead and another seven wounded, his force had proven that the aliens were not unbeatable. Their soldiers ran in the face of his overwhelming force. But the best was yet to come.

He found Staff Sergeant Wang midway up the second corridor, far enough from the combat engineers working on the next armored door to allow them to speak comfortably. "Report, Sergeant," Ping instructed.

Wang's head snapped up. He had been examining the weapon in his hand … a strange contraption very unlike the flat-black QBZ-44B assault carbine the rest of the force carried. At 950 cm in length, this device was considerably longer and fashioned from a dull silvery metal framework, with bright red coils around the long barrel and a heavy power cable and an equally heavy bracket at the bottom. This was the QBD-48 electromagnetic rifle, a man-portable railgun capable of firing a specially fabricated 12 cm steel rod at nearly two thousand meters per second, or approximately Mach 6. Of course, the phrase 'man-portable' was a stretch, since the single-use power source weighed in at 45 kg and the weapon needed to be mounted on a special tripod because the force the device generated would rip through the shoulder of any man stupid enough to attempt to fire it as if it were a normal rifle. The product of decades of research, ten of the deadly devices were deployed with his forces.

"Sir, the weapon performed well. I was able to score a hit on one of their soldiers. The projectile pierced their much-feared armor without problem," Wang announced proudly.

Ping smiled at this news, then glanced around, "And what of Hu Lun?"

Wang gestured with a nod to a body across the corridor. "Corporal Hu fired as well; I am unable to report on his accuracy."

Ping turned to see the body Wang was focused on; the head and most of the right shoulder had been cleaved off in a viscous line, cauterized by the alien's weapons and almost bloodless. Still on its tripod, the rear half of the corporal's QBD-48 showed that it had suffered the same fate. Ping grimaced – they had lost one of their precious weapons, leaving them with only nine now. "He fought bravely," Ping said solemnly but with force. Looking at the other bodies in the corridor, he added, "they all did. That is what I will report. They died so that China will live free and strong."

"Yes, sir," Wang agreed, but with less gusto.

Ping clapped the sergeant on the shoulder with a nod, then moved forward to speak with the engineers. Despite the delays, they were progressing. *And we have proven that the aliens can be beaten; in the end, they are human after all!* The success of their mission was all but guaranteed.

Terra Monitor East Asia, Terra orbit
2048APR20 23:32 UTC

"Lieutenant? A word," ENS Sofie Claussen called back to the operations officer seated at his desk.

LT Duong Van Hien stood up and pulled down on his blue uniform jacket to straighten his appearance before heading down the central aisle and stepping into the first row on the right to stand with Claussen behind one of the comms stations. "What do we have?" he asked.

Claussen looked down at the young crewman seated at the station. "Tell him."

Only one year removed from her university days in Cameroon, CRW1 Lucie Olembe answered nervously, "Sir. Lieutenant," she began, then swallowed. "We lost our connection with SCO Shanghai. They failed to report in at 23:00 and I cannot get a response now," she said in single rushed breath.

Duong looked up at the main display and checked the time. Thirty-two minutes had passed since the missed communications. "And you're telling me now?" he demanded, aiming his remarks at the two women.

Claussen stepped forward as Olembe recoiled slightly from the rebuke. With a nod to the crewman on her team, the communications officer held her ground. "She alerts Chief Ruiz. Ruiz alerts me and now I alert you. Missing a scheduled check-in or checking in late isn't unusual. Not responding when we directly contact them is. Now you're in the loop."

Duong realized his misstep; the team had followed established procedure. "And you're certain the problem isn't on our end?"

With her hands on her hips, Claussen replied, "Already checked. We have no trouble connecting with SCO Sydney or SCO Frankfurt. No problem with Terra Station either." Anticipating the lieutenant's next probable question, "We asked Sydney to contact Shanghai using ground networks, but they had no more success than we did."

"And I suppose Terra Station cannot raise them either," Duong added. Claussen nodded silently in confirmation.

Duong was the second shift duty officer for the orbital platform. East Asia was one of six (and in the future, ten) monitor stations that were built in response to two early incursions of near-Earth space. Rather than tie up valuable starships to defend the planet below, the Commonwealth built powerful orbital defense platforms to ring the homeworld. Despite having double the fire power of the Fleet's large heavy cruisers, the monitors could be produced for a fraction of the cost since they didn't require all the infrastructure needed around the powerful StarDrive units that allowed the Fleet's starships to span the vast distances between stars.

Unlike Terra Station, which maintained a geostationary orbit some thirty-five thousand kilometers above Terra at the intersection of the equatorial plane and the prime meridian, the monitors were designed to operate in an active geosynchronous orbit at a much lower altitude. Monitor East Asia was positioned above Mongolia, placing eastern Russia, China, Japan, Korea and most of Southeast Asia under its watchful eye. Their communications with Commonwealth facilities on the planet's surface was not based on standard radio, but on advanced Commonwealth technology that was supposed to be far more reliable. *So, what was the problem?*

Duong glanced again at the time. *She probably isn't asleep yet*, he assured himself. *Better to do it now than wait until she is*. He looked down to Olembe, "Give me a channel to the commander."

The crewman touched a few controls on her console, then looked up as a voice responded from the nearby speaker, "Jefferson here."

Duong breathed a sigh of relief that voice did not sound groggy. "Apologies for the late hour, Commander. But we have a situation."

There was an audible sigh before CDR Jefferson answered, "I'm on my way."

Terra Station, Terra orbit
2048APR20 23:47 UTC

Jiang Weijia closed the book she was reading and was about to go into her bedroom when the tone sounded at her door. Reluctantly, the Director of Defense turned instead to see why someone was calling on her at such a late hour. Touching a control, the door opened to reveal a pair of familiar faces. "Admiral, Captain. I assume this is a matter of some urgency," she stated, then stood to the side. "Please, come in."

"Thank you, Director," VADM Erin Fitzpatrick responded as she availed herself of Jiang's hospitality.

"My apologies for the time," CAPT Grachus added as he followed the senior officer into the room and stood to her side.

"Not at all," Jiang reassured the commander of the space station. She gestured towards the sitting area. "Would you care to have a seat?"

Fitzpatrick stood in front of the large display mounted opposite the sitting area, "I think it best if we remain standing, ma'am." Grachus followed the admiral's lead.

Before Jiang could question this, a new tone sounded, this time from the display. "Now? Who can this be?" the director wondered aloud.

"That should be Ms. Tanaka," Fitzpatrick answered flatly. "I asked Commander Guan to arrange a channel for this discussion."

LCDR Guan was the commanding officer of the Solar Commonwealth's office in New York, as Jiang recalled. The same office that the Regent's chief of staff was operating from this week. *Curiouser and curiouser*, Jiang thought. She touched a control on the wall next to the display and was rewarded with an image of the seal of the Regent's office along with text confirming the source of transmission was indeed SCO New York. "Answer," she instructed the system, and the original image faded away, replaced by Tanaka Chie standing in an office, presumably on the west side of Manhattan. "Ms. Tanaka," Jiang began, then turned to face Fitzpatrick, "Admiral, are we expecting any more people?"

"No, ma'am," Fitzpatrick returned with a slight grin. "And as Captain Grachus has already stated, we apologize for the short notice, but I need to advise both of you of a serious issue that was just brought to my attention." She paused for only a heartbeat, "We have lost contact with the office in Shanghai."

Tanaka shook her head, seeming confused. "And?" she questioned the senior-most officer in the defense forces.

Jiang, however, immediately grasped the admiral's point, "Where is the Regent?"

"Terra Base Australia," Fitzpatrick replied quickly, and with a certain relief. This passed just as fast, "But I'm ordering him transported immediately to Terra Station."

On the display, Tanaka exploded, "What? Why? Would someone tell me what's going on?"

Since Fitzpatrick had arranged the meeting, Jiang yielded to her to provide her reasoning with a small hand gesture she hoped was outside the range of the camera transmitting their image to New York.

"Loss of contact with SCO Shanghai cannot be explained. Since this office is currently the Regent's residence on Terra, precautions dictate that we secure him from any potential dangers." She stated this slowly, trying to couch the threat in neutral tones.

"What danger?" Tanaka persisted. "You just confirmed that he's not in Shanghai. He's in Australia. In the middle of our most secure base."

Fitzpatrick shook her head, "Until a few minutes ago, we thought the same thing about Shanghai. Until we know what's going on there, we cannot say which sites are secure. We have to consider the entire planet a potential risk."

"Really? Based on what?" Tanaka shot back. "You just admitted you don't know why Shanghai won't respond. What makes Terra Station any safer than Australia?"

Fitzpatrick was growing frustrated. "Believe me, it's not my first choice. I'd rather send him to *Intrepid*, but she's in Mars orbit at the moment." She stared straight at the image of the chief of staff. "*Enterprise* is in Alpha Centauri; *Valiant* is halfway to Sirius. Given that, Terra Station will have to do."

Tanaka folded her arms, "I think you are overreacting, Admiral."

"She is not," Jiang declared. While she respected Tanaka Chie and considered her a valuable advisor to the Regent, the woman had no military training and could not be expected to understand the position the admiral was in. "The admiral is acting to protect the Regent and the Commonwealth from an unknown threat. Just as I would have when I held her position."

Erin tried to remain unmoved by that endorsement. "It is simply a question of priorities. First, we must secure the Regent; then we can investigate the issue in Shanghai and determine how to deal with it."

Tanaka nodded, "I understand. I of course defer to your wisdom on such military matters," she agreed. "But be warned – he isn't going to like it."

Fitzpatrick smiled and then tried to hide that reaction, "Believe me, I know. But that's another reason to bring him here to the station. He can yell at me to his heart's content. At least he'll be alive to enjoy all that yelling."

Now it was Tanaka's turn to hide her smile. But as that passed, she turned serious again, "There is another matter. As I recall, Ms. Quintilius remained in Shanghai after the Regent departed for Australia."

That information caused Jiang to look quickly to Fitzpatrick, who nodded subtly in response. "Yes," the director agreed, drawing the word out. "That does complicate matters."

Terra Base Australia, Queensland, Australia
2048APR21 10:07 AEST (2048APR21 00:07 UTC)

The group moved from an office into the larger hangar as GCAP Eiriksdatter continued. "And these are the F-2 *Arrow*," she declared, guiding the party between two aerospace craft strategically positioned on either side of the open doorway; a red runner led further into the vast chamber, no doubt the path they were expected to take as they toured the facility. "With more power and better designed for atmospheric flight, these have replaced the older *Darts* as our first line of defense."

The Regent smiled and nodded politely, hoping he looked sufficiently impressed. He certainly didn't want to bring any attention to the fact that the F-1 *Darts* the group captain was so quick to dismiss had been his idea and Professor von Reiner's design thirty years ago; a solution to the question of how to counter the numerous air forces of the world by a distant branch of humanity that had more experience with spaceflight than they did with aerial combat. Instead, he responded, "Yes. I believe two of these craft were my escort down from Shanghai this morning."

Eiriksdatter beamed, "Yes, sir. Lieutenants Dulabi and Alagiah from 22nd Squadron. Two of our finest."

The Regent nodded, "Well, they certainly did an excellent job this morning. Please thank them for me." He made a point of bending close to examine the right-side fin on the *Arrow* closer to him. *Yes*, he admitted, *it's definitely different from the old F-1.* He nodded again as he pursed his lips, hoping that would convince the assembled officers that he had a clue as to what he was looking at. *Smile and nod*, he reminded himself. *Smile and nod.*

After a nearly hour-long tour of the Solar Base Operations Center, the commodore had turned the group over to Eiriksdatter for the Solar Flight portion of the program. According to the agenda, this would be followed by a tour of the base medical facility before joining a select group for lunch. A part of him wondered what would happen during the two-hour session the brigadier had requested for Solar Guard after lunch. *What is Kang going to do,* he pondered, *stage a mock invasion of New Zealand?*

The Regent was so engrossed in his own thoughts that he missed the captain's attempts to move him on to the next display. "Sir? If you'll follow me, we'd like to show you the prototype for the new C-9 transport," Eiriksdatter gently urged the leader of the Commonwealth. "It's quite impressive."

"Of course, Captain," the Regent returned, embarrassed that he had been caught daydreaming. *I have to make sure Argenta doesn't hear about this*, he chided himself when movement out of the corner of his eye distracted him.

A young officer in Base blue hurried towards Hamed, the two exchanging a few brief words in hushed tones before the commodore nodded and moved to stand by the Regent. She addressed the group, "My apologies everyone, but we are going to have to cut this short." Lowering her head and her voice, she added for the Regent's ears only, "Sir, I need you to come with me right now."

The Regent mirrored the commodore's whisper, "Why? What's wrong?"

Hamed placed a hand on the Regent's arm, which drew an immediate reaction from the two closest agents on his security detail. A subtle headshake from their boss convinced the man and woman to stand down – this was not a threat to their principal. As Hamed tried to quietly guide the leader of humanity away from the group, she explained, "There's been an incident."

The black ground car screeched to a halt a few meters from the waiting shuttlecraft. Nothing happened until the two identical cars following the first took up position on either side of the first; only then did a squad of grey-suited security agents spill out of the chase cars and form a cordon leading from the first car to the shuttlecraft's open hatch.

Dressed identically to the rest of her agents, LT Krejci stepped forward and released the lock on the door of the lead car, finally allowing the Regent to exit the vehicle. She ushered the man at a brisk pace to his waiting craft in silence. Once he was safely in the shuttlecraft and the door closed, she gestured for her team to fall back to their vehicles to allow the spacecraft to lift off.

Inside, the Regent came to an abrupt stop, looking around in confusion. "I think I left my tablet in the car," he explained absently.

"Not to worry sir," SGT Amani answered, reaching into a compartment and retrieving an identical device. She handed this to the Regent, "that's why we carry the backup. I'm sure Lieutenant Krejci will locate the other one and secure it."

"Yes. Thank you, Fasha," the Regent started, accepting the replacement device and trying to hide his embarrassment. "I'm sure the luggage didn't make it back in time either. It doesn't matter." He began to move down the aisle towards his seat, "Let's just get in the air and get back to Shanghai. In what? Forty minutes again?"

"Uh, sir?" Amani stumbled as she tried to correct the Regent. "Our orders are to take you to Terra Station."

The Regent spun about on those words. "Yes. But after going to Shanghai. We have to get … our people." He wanted to say "Argenta" but even now felt compelled not to. She hated it when he referred to her as his consort or partner, and ever since she stepped down as Executive Director, she refused any sort of official treatment. As she once phrased it in terms *he* could understand, "she was damned if she was going to be First Lady of the Commonwealth!"

None of this was known to the sergeant, though. "I'm sorry, sir. As far as I know, our destination is Terra Station." She gestured to the waiting seat in hopes the Regent would secure himself for takeoff.

Instead, the Regent's hand involuntarily formed a fist that he had to consciously relax. "Where is the pilot?" he demanded through gritted teeth.

Amani had never seen the Regent this agitated. She stepped back and lifted the handset from the wall, speaking softly. Seconds later, the cockpit door opened and FLT Svetlana Akinshina stepped out.

"Is there a problem, sir?" the diminutive Russian asked.

"Yes," the Regent insisted and stepped forward to stand centimeters from the pilot. Uncharacteristically, he ignored the fact that in the cramped quarters of the shuttlecraft he towered over the much younger woman. Right now, the man was angry, and chivalry be damned. "I need you to take us to Shanghai. Now." The tone in his voice made it clear that this matter was not open to debate.

To her credit, Akinshina didn't blink; she didn't flinch. "No, sir. My orders are to take you directly to Terra Station. Admiral Fitzpatrick was quite clear on that."

"I don't care who gave you those orders. I'm giving you *new* orders," the Regent countered, the menace in the words implicit.

"I understand, sir. The Admiral also addressed that. I am to ignore any protest or threat you might make." For a brief instance, the lieutenant softened, "I'm sorry."

The Regent took a deep breath, "Who is the co-pilot today?"

Akinshina kept her head high, "Sublieutenant Lacerda, sir. And I should warn you, he received the same orders. Directly from the admiral."

The Regent closed his eyes and tried to calm the storm building. "Lacerda; yes. Good man," he admitted, then began to nod, "I understand. You are all just following orders. I'm ... sorry." He whispered the last part.

"Of course, sir," Svetlana returned, happy to believe the conflict had passed. "If you'll take your seat, we can be on our way."

"Yes," he agreed, then turned towards his seat, "And again, I'm ..." but he never completed the thought. Instead, he secured himself in the chair just as he felt the gentle change in gravity as the shuttlecraft floated into the air and with a slight jolt rocketed skyward.

From the overhead speakers, Akinshina's voice returned, "Sir, Shuttlecraft *Erin* is on course for Terra Station. ETA, forty-four minutes."

The Regent said nothing in reply. Instead, he pondered his next move. There was no point in acting against the flight crew – as he'd just admitted, they were following orders their superiors issued. *No*, he thought as he activated the tablet in his lap, though his eyes never focused on the surface of the device. *If anything happens to Argenta, I'm going to kill Erin. I just don't know how yet.* It wasn't a malevolent threat; it was a promise he made to himself.

CHAPTER 5

Commonwealth Office (level 14), Shanghai, PRC
2048APR21 08:14 CST (2048APR21 00:14 UTC)

CAPT Ranbir Singh opened the stairwell door to find the corridor on this level in chaos. He jumped back quickly to avoid being knocked down by a Sentry in full armor as the woman bounded into the stairwell and down the next flight of stairs. As she passed, a tinny "Sorry" came from a speaker on the underside of her helmet.

Trying again, Singh was able to make it halfway down the corridor when he nearly collided with a Base security guard as the guard hurried out of an open doorway. "Coming through," the man blurted as he tried to pass Singh.

The captain caught the guard's arm, "Crewman, where can I find Lieutenant Hale?"

The man looked up startled, finally registered the face of the person he nearly bowled over. "Sorry, sir. He should be in Ops." When Singh failed to release his arm, the crewman added, "End of the corridor, turn right."

"Thank you, Crewman," the captain said loudly, making a show of finally removing his hand from the younger man's arm. The crewman resumed his course, disappearing into another room five meters down the corridor and across from the first.

Singh followed the directions and located his destination as promised. With the door to the operations office already open, he stepped inside and called out to the crowded room, "Lieutenant Hale?"

"Yeah?" a frustrated voice returned from the front of the room. "What is it?" the man continued as he extricated himself from his entourage. Recognizing the visitor, Hale became a little more deferential, "Captain. I thought you were staying on twenty-six."

"I tried to contact you, but I couldn't get through," Singh explained.

Hale sighed, "We've been a little busy." The operations officer continued to glance around at his people in the room rather than focus on Singh.

The captain understood Hale's frustration. The lieutenant was Solar Base, responsible for the day-to-day operations of this office; Singh was Commonwealth Security, responsible for the protection of the Regent and his staff. Neither of them had any experience with a situation like this, and no one wants to hear another department point out that fact when you're dealing with the crisis.

"I need an update," Singh explained. "I have eight agents upstairs; how can we help?"

Hale shook his head, "The Sentries are calling the shots. Ensign Barzini has nine of her own people, but Mackenzie says she can't use them. Not yet at least."

Now it was Singh shaking his head, "So we're just supposed to sit around and wait? The Sentries have what? Twenty-five people? Twenty-three now without Chu and the one that was wounded."

"Twenty-two," Hale corrected. "Another Sentry was wounded a few minutes ago."

"Twenty-two," Singh repeated. "Combined, our people could double the Sentries' numbers." Singh paused to let that sink in, then asked, "Why not talk to Mackenzie again?"

Hale thought about it for a moment, then nodded, "Why not." He gestured for Singh to follow him as he moved towards a small room portioned off from the rest of the operations office by a wall of glass. Closing the door reduced the noise from the group in ops considerably.

Touching a control on the desk display, he adjusted the screen angle to give Singh a clear view. The face of a woman in a green uniform appeared. "Leepkai," she answered.

Hale took charge, "Corporal, I need to speak with Sergeant Mackenzie."

Leepkai's eyes darted between the two men on her display. "The sergeant isn't in CIC right now, Lieutenant," she explained.

"Just connect me, Corporal," Hale insisted.

Leekpai considered her options, then yielded. "Yes, sir," she answered, and her face disappeared from the display, replaced by a series of distorted images until at last, SGT Mackenzie appeared.

From the closeup image and odd multi-colored lighting, it was clear that the image of the sergeant was provided by the helmet of her armored suit. "What is it, Lieutenant?" she began, then noticed the second face. "Captain?"

Singh jumped in, hoping to take some of the Sentry's obvious frustration away from Hale (after all, it was his idea to call), "Sergeant, where are you right now? And where are the hostiles?"

Mackenzie was not impressed by the question, "I'm on level three and the enemy is on sub-level one right now. And Corporal Leekpai could have told you that."

That bad already? Singh thought. Containment wasn't working; once the hostiles made it to ground level, the Sentries would be forced to defend two stairwells, plus the lifts. Another thought occurred, "Sergeant, isn't there an armory on sub-level two?" In his mind, Singh pictured black clad invaders now equipped with the Sentries' Type 3 PPG ... or worse.

Mackenzie smiled briefly, "Don't worry. My people carried away all they could, then sealed the armory to protect the rest. They're not getting through the armory door with that little blowtorch of theirs. And if they do, the room's rigged to blow if they don't have my personal code to disarm the charges."

"Good thinking," Singh approved.

"All part of the service," Mackenzie replied. "Now if there's nothing else ..."

Singh wasn't done. "Sergeant, between Base security and my protective detail, we have nineteen trained people who could be helping you right now. Why not let us?"

Mackenzie rolled her eyes, having had this discussion with ENS Barzini already. "First, because your people don't have the right training, and my people don't have the time to retrain you. You're trained to arrest someone or to shield the Regent; we're trained for combat."

"We can all fire a weapon," Singh persisted. "And you're taking casualties. We can't just keep falling back up the building – you'll run out of Sentries before we run out of floors."

"Well, the other problem is: you don't have any armor," the Guard woman countered. "Without it, your folks will be shredded by automatic weapons fire, and my people will be killed trying to save them. That's not helping."

"What about the armor Fourth Platoon left behind?" Hale argued. "We could use that." Because the other Guard platoon had travelled to a Commonwealth base, there was no reason for them to carry their armor with them.

Mackenzie smirked, "Guard armor isn't like an emergency environment suit; it isn't one size fits all." She sighed, thinking, *I really don't have time for this.* "Our armor is custom fit to each individual. So, unless your people are doppelgängers for Captain Bruttius and the rest of Fourth Platoon, those suits aren't going to fit." She paused for a moment, then yielded, "But you know what … you're welcome to try. Maybe some of you can find a match or two in that pile. I'm sure the captain won't mind. But you'll have to supply your own weapons – I've already raided Fourth Platoon's reserve cache for my own people."

Singh smiled at last, "Sounds like a plan, Sergeant." He turned to looked at Hale, who nodded agreement. "One more thing. Do we know yet how many hostiles we're dealing with?"

Mackenzie grimaced at that, "At least ninety or so, but it looks like they have plenty of reserves."

Singh turned to Hale in confusion. The Base officer explained, "They know enough to knock out our sensors as they secure each level. We've never seen more than ninety at any one time, but even after the Sentries inflict casualties, the number remains around the same when they reach the next level."

"How many casualties?" the captain inquired.

"We only have two wounded right now," Mackenzie reported with some pride. "We've killed over thirty of the enemy and wounded at least that many, probably more."

As a security officer, Singh was appalled by those numbers. And a little surprised that the sergeant didn't seem fazed at all. *Mackenzie is right*, he realized. *We're not trained for combat.*

"Sirs, if there's nothing else, I do have a *siege* I need to stop," Mackenzie reminded the two officers, pulling Singh from his thoughts.

"Of course, Sergeant. Good luck," Hale returned. Mackenzie didn't wait for Singh to follow the lieutenant's lead before closing the channel on her end. The display turned black. He moved towards the door and opened it. "Barzini," he called out into the room.

The ensign sprinted over and stood just outside the door, "Sir?"

Hale nodded towards the security service captain, "Go with Captain Singh. I want you to find out if the Guard armor will fit any of your people." He looked around the room, "Anything that will help us hold out until relief arrives."

Barzini brightened at those words, "Do we know when that will be?"

Singh stepped past Hale, causing the ensign to step back. "Not yet. But they are coming. That I can guarantee." He walked along the back wall of the operations office, then turned, "Come along, Ensign. Let's go find a suit of armor in your size."

Terra Monitor East Asia, Terra orbit
2048APR21 00:36 UTC

CDR Abigail Jefferson studied the image on her display, frustrated that there was so little detail each time she zoomed in for a closer look. With communications between the monitor station and SCO Shanghai cut off, she was limited to what their small network of satellites could see from orbit. And that network was designed to monitor for aircraft and missiles; they were not spy satellites intended to watch people on the ground. At best, they could detect convoys of trucks in open country, not a single passenger vehicle winding through a congested city.

The image on the main display was focused on the immediate area around the Commonwealth office, which periodically turned white as intervening clouds floated over the city and blocked the satellite's vantage point. That alone caused Jefferson to suspect a man-made cause to the comms breakdown – it seemed very convenient that the local blackout and interference with communications would coincide with increased cloud cover. That was too much of a coincidence. "Any luck?" the commander demanded.

"No, ma'am," ENS Claussen returned. "We've been through the full spectrum four times now. There is still no response from Shanghai to our hails."

Jefferson rubbed her temples in exhaustion, then turned her head to look across the room. "Lieutenant Ortiz. Send them in."

"Yes, ma'am," FLT Ortiz responded, her red Solar Flight uniform setting her apart from the sea of Solar Base blue in the operations center. She was executive officer for the 12th Interceptor Squadron and served as the control officer for the squadron's pilots. Tapping an icon on her console, she advised, "Alpha Flight, you are clear for launch."

"Copy, Sky Dragon," SLT Concepcion replied.

On her console display, Ortiz watched as the hangar doors slid open on the underside of the space station. Once the doors were twenty meters apart, two F-1 *Darts* dropped through the opening, their stubby fins setting them apart from their newer F-2 brethren. As one, the two craft banked and accelerated away from the station.

Concepcion's voice returned, "Red Falcon Alpha, flight of two, away at zero-zero-three-eight-one-nine Zulu."

"Red Falcon Alpha, go sensors active; maintain telemetry," Ortiz ordered. The mission of this flight was to provide the station and the other Commonwealth forces with visuals and details of the situation around the Shanghai office. "Go weapons live; use of force is authorized. Confirm," Ortiz followed.

CDR Jefferson and the SLDR Karim, the squadron's CO, had discussed this earlier and decided that, given the current mystery, it would be prudent to allow the interceptors to use force to defend themselves rather than waiting for confirmation from the station. This was critical if the two pilots found themselves cut off from the rest of the Commonwealth as the office was now.

"Falcon-Four, weapons live," Janella Concepcion confirmed.

"Falcon-Seven, weapons live," her partner, ENS Seweryn, echoed.

Ortiz checked off one more item, then instructed, "Proceed to objective. Maintain minimum safe altitude of nine hundred meters."

"M-S-A nine-zero-zero. Confirm," Concepcion replied. "Falcon Alpha descending."

"Red Falcon Alpha, Fly High!" Ortiz offered, then muted her microphone. Turning to look across the room, "Commander, Red Falcon Alpha is on track."

"Thank you, Lieutenant," Jefferson answered. "Miss Claussen, give us visuals from Falcon Alpha. Let's see what they see." Two windows opened on the main display, showing the view from the two fighters as they dove to the planet below.

Terra Station, Terra orbit
2048APR21 00:54 UTC

The first face the Regent saw when he stepped out of shuttlecraft *Erin* was her namesake, VADM Fitzpatrick. Jerking his thumb back to the small craft behind him, he ordered, "I want this thing turned around and sent back to Shanghai. We need to get Argenta out of there!"

Where others may have been cowed by this outburst, the admiral chose not to be. "We will, sir. In time."

"Was there something vague about my order, Admiral. Now!" the Regent bellowed, no longer interested in who might overhear him dressing down the top-ranking officer in the Commonwealth in the middle of the landing bay. *Rank hath its privileges, and no one out-ranks me!*

Fitzpatrick wasn't backing down either. "Sir, until we know more about the situation, no shuttles are going anywhere near Shanghai. Right now, Miss Quintilius is secure within our facility; any attempt to transport her could expose her to greater risk, not less."

The Regent was ready to argue that they send a fighter but stopped when he remembered that none of the combat craft had two seats. *Where is she going to sit? She can't fly it herself. I'm letting all this rattle me,* he admitted. "And what the hell *is* the situation?" he demanded instead, heading for the door of the landing bay.

"Contact with the office was lost approximately one hour forty minutes ago. Visual scans from Terra Monitor East Asia are difficult due to local weather conditions," Fitzpatrick began as she followed him into the corridor towards the lifts.

He rounded on her. "Clouds! Just say clouds!" The doors opened at his approach, and he stepped into the lift, Fitzpatrick in tow.

"Yes, sir. Clouds," the admiral complied. "We have two fighters en route from Monitor East Asia. ETA five minutes."

The Regent digested this information as the lift car ascended. *There are my fighters*, he thought. *Maybe I should see if they can fly one back by remote control to get Argenta out of there?* He dismissed that fantasy as the lift came to a halt and the doors opened. Out the door and a short march down the corridor to reach the main defense conference room.

"I want Guard troops on standby from Australia. I want every fighter we have down there ready to go the minute we find out what's going on," the Regent's voice boomed as he entered the room.

"That has already been seen to," Jiang Weijia answered as she stood just inside the room. The Regent had to come to an abrupt stop to avoid slamming into her. With a silent look towards Fitzpatrick, Jiang instructed the admiral to take her place at the conference table. At the same time, Jiang lowered her voice to address the leader of the Commonwealth. "Regent, may I have a word?" The fact that this was not really a question became evident as Jiang grasped the Regent's arm to guide him back out of the room.

Despite her smaller stature, the director of defense achieved her goal. Once the conference room doors closed, she addressed the Regent in still hushed tones. "Sir, as Miss Quintilius is not available, I feel compelled to act in her stead. You need to control your emotional outbursts."

The Regent seethed at the mention of his dearest love, then choked as he heard the director's words repeated in Argenta's voice. *That's exactly what she would tell me*, he admitted. If she were here. *If she ever finds out what I've been doing to save her*, he admitted, *she'll kill me*.

"Yes," he agreed softly. "Yes," a little louder this time. "I … uh. I … I'm sorry."

"There is no need for apologies, Regent," Jiang replied evenly. "Nor is there any reason that we need mention this to Miss Quintilius on her return. So long as you can control your emotions."

The Regent looked into the eyes of the woman he'd known for thirty years. His trusted adviser on all matters concerning the defense of the Commonwealth. "Are you absolutely sure you're not Vulcan?"

Jiang's eyes drew subtly cooler, her voice colder. "We have discussed this," she reminded him. The Regent feared he may have overstepped, but the moment passed. "We should return to the conference room."

"Yes. Yes, you're right," the Regent readily agreed, happy to have dodged yet another bullet. *I have got to learn to keep my mouth shut.*

He found the usual suspects gathered around the conference table as he moved to take his customary seat at the head. Agnete Lindfjeld, the executive director of the Commonwealth and the designated head of his government, sat to his right. Jiang sat on the right of Lindfjeld, then Director of Security Fabius followed by Director of Finance Ramana to complete the civilian side. Opposite them were Fitzpatrick and MGEN Graham of the Guard nearest to the Regent, with Base RADM Derbez and Flight CDRE Bombe completing the military group. He also noted a display positioned to the right of Ramana to allow his chief of staff to participate remotely.

"People," the Regent began, always conscious not to go with his first instinct, which was to say *Gentlemen.* "Where do we stand?"

Erin Fitzpatrick touched a control, and the oversized display at the opposite end of the table lit up, revealing three distinct images. In the center was a detailed map of the area of Shanghai immediately surrounding the Commonwealth office. Unfortunately, the map was severely lacking in useful details like people and vehicles at the moment. To either side were what the Regent assumed were live images from the nose cameras of the two fighters the admiral had mentioned earlier. The images alternated from distant views of the ground below to walls of white, no doubt as the fighters passed through layers of clouds. All in all, impressive sights, but not very helpful.

"We should have visual of the area in two minutes," Bombe informed them.

The Regent nodded, "What do we have from the Chinese?"

Marcellus Fabius took that one, "We have had several discussions with Beijing, all to no avail. They insist there is a massive blackout across the city, which is hampering their ability to address our concerns."

"And the communications problems?" the Regent followed.

"They claim to be suffering from the same problem, which is one of the main reasons it is taking so long to make any progress," Fabius replied. "They have even questioned if our office could be the cause, saying the communications failures appear to be centered on its location." The director raised a suspicious eyebrow to that last statement but was obligated to relay the information as he received it.

The Regent was under no such obligation. "Well, that's bullshit," he declared flatly. He looked around the table, "Sorry, ladies."

"I've heard worse," Prudence Graham announced. "From you, sir."

"Who hasn't?" Agnete seconded. A subdued chuckle ran around the table.

The Regent grinned for the first time in quite a while. "Yes, well. I still don't believe them." He looked to the image of his chief of staff, "Chie, arrange a video call with President Wu. If the man's going to lie to me, let him at least do it to my face."

"Yes, sir," a tinny voice answered.

"What about what we can detect outside the area. My first instinct is to suspect the locals, but is it possible this is caused by some outside nation or group?"

"Do you mean terrorists?" Fabius questioned, as usual showing his disdain for the very concept. It was a phenomenon unique to the planet below; there was no equivalent in the Terran Enclave where most of the senior staff were born and raised. On the distant Ssenn-controlled planet of Sserllich-Haash Four, a branch of humanity had grown and flourished in a peace enforced on them by their alien benefactors. These humans understood laws and the need for police; they even understood war as it had been fought by their ancestors. But the idea of an organized, non-state group attacking civilians indiscriminately? That was something they learned of on Earth. "I suppose, but it seems unlikely. As I understand it, the Chinese are *very* good at suppressing these types of groups. Also, interfering with our communications would require technology far in advance of what is available on planet."

"All right. What about other nations? The Americans or the Russians?" the Regent countered.

"It is more likely the Americans would focus on New York, not Shanghai," Jiang declared. "The Russians are a possibility, but I cannot see a motive. Indeed, I cannot attribute a motive to any of the major nations of Terra. How does this action benefit them?"

"Neither can I," the Regent admitted, "but something is causing this; I cannot believe it is just a simple malfunction."

Fitzpatrick nodded. "Let's see what we learn from the fighters."

CHAPTER 6

Commonwealth Office (level 5), Shanghai, PRC
2048APR21 08:57 CST (2048APR21 00:57 UTC)

"Sergeant, they're almost through door A-zero-three-nine," a voice announced in her helmet.

Time's up, Mackenzie admitted to herself. "Fall back to level ten. All troops."

"Sarge, I can try to hold them from the landing. Buy you some time," a new voice countered.

Heather lashed out, "Harper, move! Now! That's an order." The sergeant was in no mood to put up with any of the private's Franklin bravado. *What does she think this is*, Mackenzie wanted to scream, *a God-damned video game?* She made a note to upbraid Private Harper for that little stunt in front of the entire platoon once this was all over. Assuming they both survived.

"Sergeant? You're not going to try to hold level five?" LTJG Hale's voice asked.

Mackenzie couldn't remember if they had already had this conversation, so she didn't bite the officer's head off. "Lieutenant, after level three, we don't have security doors in the stairwells until you get to level ten." Once the invaders reached the ground level, Mackenzie was forced to split her troops between two stairwells. And with four of her Sentries wounded now, she was dealing with a depleted platoon. Luckily, they were able to use the lift cars to block the two shafts that ran the height of the building, or they would have to split their forces even further. "We only have fire doors between levels four and nine, and their demo charges will blow right through those."

"What about the annex?" Hale persisted.

The ten-story residential annex stood in the shadow of the thirty-story main building. Fortunately, the two buildings were independent and did not connect at ground level or below. Fortunate because the fusion reactor that provided both buildings with power was located below the annex and currently out of reach of the enemy. Unless they captured the walkway that connected the two buildings on the fifth level.

"We'll blow the skybridge well before they get to five," Mackenzie assured the officer.

"Were we able to evacuate everyone? I don't remember seeing more people up here," Hale asked in confusion.

Mackenzie shook her head, wondering again why the two of them were not on the same page. "No, sir. We left them in place. Once we destroy the bridge, they'll be sealed in tight, safe from the group downstairs." Mackenzie didn't add that it was still possible that the Chinese (and she knew it was the Chinese, who else could it be) might still tunnel into the annex the way they had the main building. There was no reason to worry Hale about that possibility if he didn't think of it himself.

"Then we should have moved the VIPs to the annex," Hale decided.

"Not if you want to evacuate them – there's no landing pad on the annex," Heather countered. "If any of us are getting out of here, it's from the roof on thirty."

"You're right," the lieutenant admitted, sounding exhausted. "I just … I just never considered this scenario."

"Don't worry, sir. We did," Mackenzie said with just a touch of pride. "We'll get you through it."

Major Ping studied the map on the floor as he knelt, careful to keep his head down and not offer a tempting target to an alien sniper. His men had secured the third floor only four minutes ago … second floor, he corrected himself; these aliens numbered the ground floor as zero like the British. *Arrogant imperialists!* At least the floorplans provided by their so-called experts in Department 828 were proving accurate, even if they did fail to note the reinforced doors that cut off every level from those above and below. At the current rate, they would run out of gas for the torches before the aliens ran out of stories. He considered alternating stairwells to extend their reach.

"Major, we are on the fifth floor," Captain Xu reported as he ran up, grasping a note.

"How?" Ping demanded as he struggled to his feet.

Xu thrust the note towards Ping, "The doors on five were different. The engineers were able to remove them with simple charges."

Ping smiled at receiving the first good news since they breeched the basement wall. "Move the men up both stairwells. Quickly!" He shoved the captain into action to spread the word. There was still a chance, if there were no more of those alien doors to slow their pace. They could still overrun the aliens if they moved quickly.

"Get the map," he instructed Private Long as he bounded down the corridor and into the stairwell. He took the steps two at a time, surprised to not find his men bottled up on the stairs. Finding the door blasted from its hinges, he entered the corridor and traveled fifteen meters before finding one of his troops clearing a side room. "Where are the rest of you? Where are the aliens?" he demanded.

The private came to attention immediately, "Sir, we don't know. The lieutenant thinks they abandoned this floor."

Ping looked around, then continued down the corridor. Turning a corner, he found the platoon leader in a huddle with his team leaders. The lieutenant snapped to attention when he spotted the major. "Sir."

"Where are they?" Ping repeated.

"Gone," Lieutenant Liang said confidently. "They must have known they could not defend this floor."

Ping looked about, "Then chase them. Send teams up both stairwells. Blow the doors and keep going. We will cut off their escape." When he saw Liang about to speak, he preempted any discussion. "Captain Xu will send men to sweep the floors for stragglers. I need you to be the spearhead."

"Yes, sir," Liang acknowledged. Any further words were interrupted by the sound of an explosion much louder than their breeching charges. This was followed by metal screeching and finally a crash. Both officers dashed to a nearby room to find a private staring out the large floor to ceiling windows. "What happened?" Liang demanded of his man.

The private (oddly the same one Ping located when he reached this floor) turned and shrugged, "The walkway, sir. It just fell off the building."

Ping Youxia moved closer to the window, now able to see the shorter alien building across a small plaza. Private what's-his-name was correct

– the enclosed walkway that connected the buildings was gone, no doubt its wreckage smoldered in the plaza below. *But why?* He spotted dull grey doors that remained on the far building. *Are the aliens now cowering in that building after abandoning this tower?* Or did they simply destroy the connection to deny Ping a second victory? It didn't matter to the major, his quarry was far above him still. He could sense it.

"Ignore this; it saves us from having to clear that building as well," Ping declared. Stepping in front of the lieutenant, "You have your orders. Get behind the aliens."

Alpha Flight, 12th Interceptor Squadron, 2000m over Shanghai, PRC 2048APR21 00:59 UTC

At long last, SLT Janella Concepcion had an uninterrupted view of the city below. "Falcon Alpha, reduce descent. Level at one-five-zero-zero," she ordered her partner as she eased back on her controls.

"One-five-zero-zero. Confirmed," ENS Jerzy Seweryn replied.

The flight leader checked her display, first focusing on the surrounding airspace. As expected, there were no commercial aircraft in the area, but oddly there was also an absence of military or government craft as well. She would have expected to see either PLAAF or police helicopters hovering below them, but there were none in sight.

Thumbing the comms control, she reported in, "Sky Dragon, Falcon-Four. Zero, repeat, zero local traffic."

"Understood, Falcon-Four. Proceed," Ximena Ortiz replied from her station on Terra Monitor East Asia.

"Proceeding, Sky Dragon," Concepcion answered her controller, then to Seweryn, "Falcon-Seven, proceed to level one-one-zero-zero. Separation six-zero-zero."

"Understood," her wingmate returned. Thanks to their focused gravity drive, one of the advantages the *Darts* enjoyed over local fixed-wing aircraft was the ability to hover in place. Once they reached their desired altitude, the two craft would hold position three hundred meters to the east and west of the Commonwealth tower, still well above its rooftop.

Concepcion shifted her focus to the tower and the grounds around it. Once again, she was confused. The grounds of the compound were empty, and there were no people within five hundred meters of the low fence that wrapped around the property. There were also no cars, trucks or buses on the roads below. Adjusting her camera angle, Janella was able to locate a cordon of military-style vehicles around eight hundred meters in all directions around the tower. The number of people around that circle in green army uniforms far exceeded the number of civilians they were holding back.

"Sky Dragon, are you getting this?" she asked her controller.

"Affirmative, Falcon Alpha," Ortiz answer. "Any signs of activity in the tower?"

"Falcon-Seven, shift focus to tower," Concepcion ordered. She wanted to investigate the military personnel further.

"Sky Dragon," Seweryn, responded. "Scanning west side. No signs of activity." After an extended silence, Janella heard, "That's the best I can do from this position."

"Wait one," Ortiz replied. Another silence followed until she returned, "Falcon Alpha. Revised orders. M-S-A now five-hundred meters. Minimum range to target, one-hundred meters."

Damn, that's close, Concepcion thought. But obviously her boss wanted them to get the attention of anyone in the building. "M-S-A five-zero-zero. Range one-zero-zero. Confirmed, Sky Dragon." She shifted channels, "You heard the boss, Jerzy. Let's take a closer look."

Zhongshan Park, Shanghai, PRC
2048APR21 09:06 CST (2048APR21 01:06 UTC)

Captain Yang Xiwang stood in the field, staring at the foreign compound across the clearing. She had been called out along with several other Armed Police units from the Pushi barracks. In all, nearly half of their regiment now surrounded the "black flag" tower. Yang had no idea why she was here, but that wasn't important. Her orders were clear — establish a perimeter in her assigned area and make certain that no civilians crossed into the exclusion zone. Any violators were to be detained, as were any foreigners who approached the cordon.

It did not occur to Yang to question why this particular assignment had fallen to the People's Armed Police rather than the local public security bureau. In her mind, the Shanghai police were only good for two things – registering foreign visitors and managing traffic. And given the state of traffic in this city most days, they weren't any good at the latter.

She noticed movement from the corner of her eye and turned to find one of her sergeants approaching. When he stopped in front of her, she asked, "What did they say?"

Sergeant Bo was a little older than the captain but always showed Yang the respect of her rank, "Captain, they have no explanation, but we are not the only unit affected. None of the communications are working throughout the detachment." He cast a suspicious eye to the black tower, "There is talk that *they* could be the cause. An attempt to disrupt our operations."

Yang shook her head once, "Any such attempt will fail. We do not require radios to defend the state. We will rely on the method our ancestors used for centuries. Have the sergeants select a private from each platoon to act as runner." She paused to lower her voice slightly, "Make sure they select one who has passed the physical tests. I don't want to see a bunch of sweating pigs carrying my messages to the detachment HQ."

Bo nodded agreement, "Yes, Captain. Zhou Qin is our fastest runner, but she is also our best marksman."

"Then I suggest we keep her on the line," Yang replied. "Perhaps Wu Yenching; he seems fit, and he couldn't hit a truck if he were sitting in it."

Bo smiled at that, "As you wish, Captain." The sergeant turned and hurried off to implement Yang's orders.

Alone again, Yang scanned the faces of the people milling about behind the line formed by her troops and their vehicles. The civilians were mostly elderly, probably residents from the nearby residential towers. *They have nothing else to do*, she thought. *We are interrupting their morning exercises*. Yang felt bad about that, but then considered that her troops were also supplying the locals with days of entertaining gossip. *Perhaps it's a fair trade*, she considered.

With a final scan of the crowd revealing no foreigners to report, Yang returned her attention to the building at the center of this action. There was no movement; none of the aliens appeared to be active inside their fence. Which gave her no clue as to how long they would be standing here. It really didn't matter, she guessed. And it was a nice day to spend in the park.

Standing between two clusters of retirees, LT Chu watched the line of soldiers along the portable barricade erected to keep the aunties and uncles away from the Commonwealth building. When she was finishing up her run, she was surprised to find the soldiers setting up those same barricades and herding any stragglers behind their line of control. She tried to contact the office, both with her mobile phone and then with her wristband, but both devices failed her.

While she did not understand yet why this was happening, she understood its effect on her – she was cut off from her people in the Commonwealth building. When she noticed soldiers rounding up several people of obvious European and African descent, she quickly disposed of her two devices in a trash bin. Chu knew her Chinese face would not protect her forever, so she purchased a baseball cap from a nearby stall (paying cash, nothing that could be traced) and pulled the brim low to shield her from prying eyes and surveillance cameras.

All that was at least an hour ago (she couldn't be certain since disposing of her devices). She tried to find an alternate exit from the park but held back when she saw a long queue leading to policemen checking documents at the single open gate. *Yes*, she thought sarcastically. *Nothing suspicious about any of this.*

With her avenues of escape blocked, she moved back to this side of the park, hoping to find another way to reunite with her people. There were no Sentries outside the building patrolling the grounds, leading Chu to assume the entire building was under lockdown. But why? There was no obvious threat that she could see from her vantage point; no sound of weapons fire if the danger was on the opposite side. She scanned the skies, looking for some threat from above when she glimpsed a brief flash of sunlight reflected off a surface high above the building.

Straining to make out the cause, she regretted not bringing field glasses on her run. The object in question wasn't moving, which ruled out any type of airplane and most drones. There was also no indication of a large rotor for a helicopter. That left only one solution – a Commonwealth shuttle, perhaps attempting to land. Then again, she thought and continued to sweep the sky until she found it. A second shuttle, probably at the same altitude as the first. And since neither of the craft was moving to land, maybe they were fighters sent to investigate the PAP's sudden interest in the Commonwealth building.

Suddenly, Chu Daxia didn't feel quite so alone.

Zhongnanhai, Beijing, PRC
2048APR21 09:10 CST (2048APR21 01:10 UTC)

Wu Zhongxun sat at his desk in Qinzheng Hall in a foul mood. It offended him to be summoned by the aliens, as if he were some minor functionary answering the demands of the Westerners who imposed their will on China more than one hundred years earlier. The nation had long struggled to put those days far behind, yet here he was jumping when the space station that circled above insisted that he meet with them immediately. *Intolerable!*

The only satisfaction Wu found was that if the meeting were early in the morning for him, it was even earlier for the aliens, who's space station operated on London time. That brought a subtle grin to his face as he waited for the technician to set up the computer monitor in front of his desk. He refused to go to some conference room for this conversation. If he had to speak with these most distant of *laowai*, he would do it with the full regalia of his office on display.

The technician finished her work, then handed a control to the chairman's secretary. Wu looked to Premier Guo and General Cao, who nodded; they would remain outside the view of the camera. Once the door closed behind the technician, Wu steeled himself and ordered, "Turn it on."

The monitor came to life to display the usual symbol of their alien overlords. Thanks to years of dealing with his colleagues on the Central Committee, Wu was able to hide his surprise when the image changed to reveal an all-too-familiar face.

"Chairman," the Regent greeted him without fanfare.

"Regent," Wu returned in kind.

There was a noticeable pause, as if neither man wanted to be the first to speak to avoid giving the other some advantage. Wu was perfectly willing to sit in silence for as long as it took; after all, it was the Commonwealth that asked for this meeting.

The Regent was not nearly as patient and broke the standoff, "Can you tell me what is happening in Shanghai?"

Wu sighed and made a show of opening a leather folder on his desk, reading slowly from the papers inside. "I am informed that there is failure in the power grid. It appears to affect a large portion of the old city." He closed the folder, "Hardly a matter of concern for the great Commonwealth."

The Regent was having none of it. "A power failure doesn't explain why we are suddenly unable to contact our office in Shanghai. And it doesn't explain why your soldiers are now surrounding the office."

Wu maintained his balance, "As you choose to not share your technology with us, I cannot guess to the reason it would fail you. But it is not at all unusual for the local forces to be called out to maintain order and assist those affected when there is a disaster."

"Then why are they only around our building?" the Regent demanded, his volume rising.

Wu would not be goaded. "Forces would be sent where they are needed. We do not direct these actions from the capital; have you considered contacting the Shanghai committee secretary or the mayor?"

"Mister Wu," the Regent barked. As a rule, the leader of the Commonwealth refused to make use of honorifics like 'Mr. President' or 'Your Majesty' but could normally be counted on to refer to heads of state by their title. Dropping that was an indication of just how angry he was in this instance. "I want answers! Now! And if I don't get them, I'm sending in troops to find out why!"

Wu breathed slowly, centering his mind. "China joined your Commonwealth with the understanding that you were concerned with space and the other aliens. We agreed to reduce our military in the interest of global peace." His words grew harsher, "But we never surrendered control of our people and our land. Any foreign troops will be met with the full force of the People's Liberation Army. China will never be invaded again."

The Regent's anger chilled. "China recognized the Solar Commonwealth. It recognized our authority over all nations. When our troops land, they are not foreign troops. China is part of the Commonwealth, and it always will be. No matter who is in government."

Wu ignored the implied threat.

"Enjoy your day, Chairman," the Regent added before closing the channel.

"General Secretary, was it wise to antagonize the Regent?" Guo Shuang asked as he stepped forward to stand by the desk.

"He is a man, not a god. I will not bend and scrape to him," Wu grumbled to the premier.

"He threatens to send his forces. Recall that these are the forces that defeated Russia and devastated Korea," Guo countered, looking to the general for support.

"That was years ago," the General Cao Fenghe returned.

"Yes. Their forces grow stronger and more numerous, while the PLA is a shadow of its former greatness. Our navy and rocket forces gone, our ground and air forces reduced," Guo insisted.

As a general in the PLA Ground Forces and vice chairman of the Central Military Commission, Cao could be counted on to defend the People's Liberation Army to the last. "We remain the defender of the state and the party. We were not challenged then and will not be defeated now."

Wu slapped the desk. "They cannot attack us!" When Guo looked to question this, Wu explained, "It would reveal the Commonwealth to be a lie. It would prove they are no different than the empires of the past, crushing those who challenge their power. They will not risk that." He stood with some effort. "Guo Shuang, contact the committee secretary of Shanghai. We need answers," he picked up the leather folder and waved it in the air, "much more than we have here. We must demonstrate control of this situation and deny the Regent any excuse to use his vaunted troops. Go!"

"I will see to it, General Secretary," Guo declared and left the room.

The moment the door closed behind Guo, Wu rounded on Cao, "How can this happen? I was assured the Regent would be trapped in their tower. That his capture would be a matter of hours and long before any of their forces could be alerted. Well? He is free and they are alerted now! How?"

"I cannot say, Chairman. There has been no update from the Black Tiger team," Cao answered. Unlike Guo, the vice chairman was one of the few people in the government who was aware of the secret special operations force.

"We need to end this now. The man escaped the trap," Wu decided.

Cao shook his head, "Impossible. The jamming device that prevents the aliens from calling for help also prevents us from communicating with our forces. They cannot report their progress and we cannot recall them."

Wu slammed the desk again in frustration. With the path to victory denied, his only choice was to minimize the damage of a defeat. "Withdraw the aircraft, and any support troops we can reach. Locate Sun and secure him. And General Hao; we will need to provide 'responsible parties' to distance ourselves from this misfortune."

"General Hao has no knowledge of these plans," Cao protested.

"Precisely. His denials will ring hollow; as head of the PLA's advanced weapons research, he is the obvious choice. Department 828 is using his creations, after all."

Despite his disdain for throwing other officers to the wolves, Cao understood the necessity. None of this could be lain at the door of the state. It must be seen as a rogue element. "I will begin the arrests," the general answered. "And what of the Tigers?"

Wu shook his head, slumping back into his chair. "They knew the risks."

CHAPTER 7

*Alpha Flight, 12th Interceptor Squadron, 1000m over Shanghai, PRC
2048APR21 01:11 UTC*

Concepcion's hands hovered over the controls. "Falcon-Four, descending to seven-zero-zero," she advised as her craft dropped.

"Falcon-Seven, descending to seven-zero-zero," Seweryn parroted as he followed her lead.

"Acknowledged, Falcon Alpha," Ortiz replied from Monitor East Asia. "Telemetry looks good."

Concepcion focused on the image of the office tower below as her fighter gently moved three hundred meters closer to the world below. She noticed the display glitch as the counter reached 817 m. It passed immediately, then repeated at 794 m, this time lasting longer.

"Sky Dragon, Falcon-Four experiencing comms problems," Concepcion reported.

The response she received concerned her, "… gon … con-Four … metry err …" She could not be certain that it was Ortiz's voice.

"Falcon-Sev … problems … orders," made it clear that Seweryn was also having problems.

The display flashed again, showing her altitude down to 697 m before the display went dark. *Time to abort*, Janella decided, slapping the controls to reverse her descent and hopefully return her to her previous position. She could feel the *Dart* buck, unable to decide whether to rise or fall. *Not good.*

When the display finally returned, her altitude read 826 m. It took much longer to ascend than it had to descend. But more worrying was what her now functioning sensors told her about her partner. Seweryn's *Dart* was yoyoing between 634 m and 662 m.

"Sky Dragon, Falcon-Seven is in trouble," she reported as she searched for a way to help her wingmate.

"Understood, Falcon-Four," Ortiz's replied, her voice now clear. "Be advised, we are tracking incoming aircraft, your location."

"Weapons hot," Concepcion advised her controller as she brought her shields to full power, then turned her attention to Seweryn. "Falcon-Seven, respond. Falcon-Seven, confirm orders! Go weapons hot! Respond!"

A blur out of the corner of her eye and thud drew her attention back to the sky. Something hit her craft, but what? Toggling the display revealed four fast movers inbound, but the computer refused to identify them as hostile. Hence, no warning. Confused, she had to disable the IFF and manually designate the four … now six inbound as hostile while marking Falcon-Seven as friendly. With that, her targeting computer established locks just as another blur/ping struck her *Dart*.

"Unidentified aircraft. You have entered an active Commonwealth zone. Divert now!" she ordered on the standard military frequencies. One-by-one the aircraft shot by overhead, then turned at speed to make a second pass.

"Final warning," Concepcion advised as she pivoted the *Dart* to face her attackers head on. With well-practiced ease she fired twice, picking off the two leading fighters as they closed on her, the oncoming fighters spouting trails of smoke. She watched as the two planes veered away to the river a few kilometers away and waited to spot parachutes … but none deployed. Instead, the aircraft dove straight into the waters of the Pu, exploding on impact.

So confusing was this turn of events, that Concepcion only turned away when a sudden jolt ran through her fighter and the weapons display turned into a sea of red. With no other option, she punched the controls to do the one thing the other fighters couldn't – rocket straight up one thousand meters.

"Falcon-Seven, take evasive. Repeat, take evasive," she ordered, hoping that Seweryn would hear at least part of that message. Janella studied her display, but none of it made sense. Nothing was wrong with power or targeting, but the weapon was offline. *How does a pulse cannon jam? It has no moving parts!*

"Falcon-Seven, respond," Concepcion repeated, noting he was still hovering under eight hundred meters. And then he wasn't. For some reason, the *Dart* began to rotate, losing altitude rapidly.

"Falcon-Seven report!" Concepcion yelled. As she watched Seweryn's *Dart* fall below four hundred meters she noticed four new aircraft converging on the Commonwealth tower. Low and slow. Helicopters, she realized. *They've got attack helicopters.*

More alarms sounded and her F-1 began to shudder, fighting her attempts to control the craft. A red highlight on her schematic caused her to glance to her right, where she found the cause. Through the canopy she could see the right-side fin was now missing a sizeable chunk from the forward edge, sporadic sparks issuing from the exposed internals. *How? What are they firing?* she demanded from the heavens. Another blur/ping from a glancing blow. *That wasn't a missile!*

The *Dart* continued to fight her, making any sharp maneuvers impossible. And the four remaining enemy fighters were circling, taking turns as they harassed her. She wanted to track her partner's descent, but the bastards weren't going to let her. She struggled to veer out of the path of the latest attack when she noticed one, then another of the hostiles disappeared from her display.

"Red Falcon Alpha, this is Gold Eagle Alpha. Twenty-Second Fighter, out of Australia," a new voice called over the Flight Combat channel. "Do you require assistance?"

"Eagle Alpha, Falcon-Four. I am damaged but still airworthy." She checked her display, "Falcon-Seven was hit and went down."

"We will retrieve," the other pilot replied.

"Negative, Eagle Alpha. There is some form of interference below nine-zero-zero," Concepcion insisted. She didn't want these newcomers falling to the same fate as Seweryn.

"Understood," the Eagle pilot replied. "Eagle-Five, be advised. Remain above nine-zero-zero."

"Acknowledged", another new voice responded. "Hostiles eliminated."

Concepcion breathed a sigh of relief as she spotted the F-2 *Arrow* hovering alongside her damaged *Dart*, careful not to crowd her as she tried to keep her fighter steady. "Thanks for that, Mister Eagle."

The lead Eagle pilot chuckled, "That's Flight Lieutenant Dulabi to you, Sublieutenant Concepcion. And no thanks necessary. Taking out those four bandits wasn't even a challenge."

"Four," Concepcion repeated, confused. "What about the helicopters?"

Now Dulabi was confused, "Helicopters? Where?" A second later he answered his own question, "Found them. They're at two hundred meters. I thought you said we couldn't go below nine hundred?"

"We can't, they can. I can't explain it," Janella fired back.

"Not for long, Lieutenant," Dulabi countered coldly. "Eagle-Five, keep an eye on the sky. I need a little target practice." From her vantage point, Concepcion watched as the *Arrow* pivoted to bring its nose almost straight down while maintaining its hover.

The voice of the female Eagle pilot sounded in Concepcion's helmet, "Yes, sir. Good hunting."

Commonwealth Office (level 14), Shanghai, PRC
2048APR21 09:14 CST (2048APR20 01:14 UTC)

LTJG Hale scanned the ravaged room that until twenty minutes ago was the operations office. The comms and supply staff removed all the equipment they could carry, moving it to the new ops room on level twenty-five. What they could not carry, the security team rendered inoperable with strategic application of their pulse pistols to the consoles' circuitry. Nothing that was left behind could be allowed to fall into enemy hands.

"It stinks, doesn't it," PO Velasquez commented, drawing Hale from his thoughts. With Barzini one of the three lucky security guards able to fit into the Sentry armor, Velasquez was now in charge of the six guards who remained with Hale.

"Yes," Hale replied, not entirely certain what Velasquez meant by those words. The petty officer was born and raised in the United States, and though both men were technically North Americans, their language was separated by light years. Literally. "It never occurred to me that we would have to destroy our own equipment while under siege," Hale offered.

"Yeah," Velasquez agreed. "This is just supposed to be a quiet office building. Not the American embassy in Tehran."

Hale turned to look at the man, "Tehran?"

Velasquez waved away the question, "I'll explain later, sir. We better get moving."

They moved into the corridor and turned towards the B stairwell when the floor shook, followed by a blast of hot air. Rushing towards the source of the unexplained wind, they found a conference room ablaze. In one of the transparent carbon windows, a nearly one-meter round opening was burned through to the outside, the wind feeding the fire, whipping it around.

Hale struggled to pull the door closed as the fire suppression finally engaged, raining water down on the blaze. The lieutenant abandoned the door, recognizing that he would never be able to seal the door with its frame bent by the impact that caused all this damage. He glanced out the surviving windows, through the smoke and droplets, and was able to make out the shape of some rotary aircraft when it flashed a bright light, and the building again rocked.

A voice called from the overhead speakers in the corridor, "We have fires on twelve."

After another few seconds the rush of water in the conference room turned to a trickle and the fire reasserted itself, though far smaller than before. With a flash of insight, Hale understood. Their building might have an independent energy source, but water was pumped to them through the city's infrastructure. With no electricity, the pumps that supplied the area were idle. Their building maintained a reserve in a cistern on the roof, but apparently the fire sprinklers just exhausted that. Now the fires would just have to burn themselves out.

Hale sprinted to the lifts, where a comms station hung on the wall. Stabbing the all-call button, he ordered, "Fires on twelve and fourteen. All personnel evac to fifteen, then move to twenty. Now!" He released the button and turned to Velasquez, "Let's go."

"Sir?" the petty officer answered as they moved briskly to the closer stairwell A. "What about the fires? I'm pretty sure fire travels *up* a building."

Hale did not break stride, "The building isn't flammable; only the furniture is. The fires will burn out once they consume those; it won't spread into the corridors if the doors hold."

The building rocked again, followed by another announcement, "Fires on fifteen." Then a second voice (Peraza, Hale realized), "All personnel. Bypass fifteen. Move directly to twenty."

Throwing the stairwell door open, Hale squeezed into the stream of personnel moving up the stairs. When he reached the landing, he stopped as the windows revealed a black helicopter hovering only one hundred or so meters from the building. If it fired, he realized, dozens of his people in this stairwell would die. Before he could order those around him to get to the other stairwell, a bolt of lightning shattered the rotary craft and its burning wreckage fell into the streets below.

Thanking whatever god had spared him, Hale resumed his ascent.

When he finally reached the new ops room on level twenty-five, Hale walked straight to the security technician seated at the improvised defense station. "Nice shooting, Mila."

Crewman Lezhneva, turned in her chair, surprised by the operations officer's words, "Sir?"

"The helicopter," Hale explained. "You saved a lot of lives in the stairwell, including mine." When he saw the woman still was confused by his praise, he continued, "When you shot down that helicopter a minute ago." The office tower was equipped with four point-defense cannons on the roof top to defend any shuttle approaching the landing pad, as well as to discourage any aircraft from attempting an unauthorized visit.

Lezhneva shook her head slowly, "Sir, we have not fired on the helicopters. I can't make the targeting system lock on. Those shots weren't from us; they came from much higher."

Hale was more confused. "Who?" he asked of no one.

"The hand of God protects us," Velasquez announced as he clapped Hale on the shoulder.

The operations officer looked to his security chief, "I doubt very much that God uses a pulse cannon." *But I can't be certain*, he admitted to himself.

Commonwealth Office (level 9), Shanghai, PRC
2048APR21 09:15 CST (2048APR21 01:15 UTC)

Unlike Hale, Major Ping immediately recognized the source of the tremors that ran through the building. His air support had entered the fray, and they would only do that for specific reasons. The aliens must have attempted to land reinforcements on the building's rooftop helipad!

This is taking too long, his mind screamed as the building shook again. They had lost the element of surprise; the invaders from the stars would not be deterred for long. He needed to move quickly if he was to capture the target. He grabbed Lieutenant Ma by his shoulder. "How much longer?" he demanded.

Ma yelled his answer over the sound of the torch carving the door that prevented them from reaching the twelfth floor, "Almost through." He pointed down the corridor, "It's taking longer in the other stairwell; they ran out of gas and sent for a fresh tank."

The sound of the torch disappeared, and a heavy clang followed three thuds as the breeching team battered in the severed center to the door. Even before the metal cooled, two soldiers leapt through the narrow opening, peering up the stairwell in anticipation of ray guns shooting from above.

"Sir, I hear movement above us," the lead corporal called back.

"Get after them," Ping shouted, "Catch them!" He turned to the non-com behind him, "Sergeant Li, more men. Whatever it takes, I need you to catch them before they can block our advance again. Go!" He stepped back to allow the line of soldiers to follow their comrades into the maw. *Whatever it takes,* he repeated in his head. It didn't matter; he'd lost more than sixty men already. He didn't bother counting the wounded; if they were not dead, they could still hold a rifle and fight. It didn't matter if two hundred died as long as his objective was met.

Ping lost track of how many men rushed past him. Even as the whine of alien weapons fire mixed with the staccato of his own troops' response, the flow of soldiers never slowed. These were good men; the best China had. They would not fail him.

Four minutes later, Ping struggled as he climbed over the bodies of the fallen on the stairs. None of the bodies wore the strange plastic suits of the enemy; all were dressed as he was.

Reaching the fifteenth floor, he stepped into the corridor only to find more of his fallen troops. Down the corridor, Liang waved at him while standing over yet another body.

"What is it?" Ping demanded testily of his subordinate. There was much to do, and Ping was wasting his time counting the fallen.

"Sir, look," he insisted, pointing the crumpled body on the floor. "She's not one of ours."

Ping's eyes followed Liang's direction, finally registering the form at his feet. Liang was right, what he assumed was a black uniform was in fact a dark blue coverall, while the lack of any helmet revealed dirty blonde hair pulled back in a loose braid. He expected the first alien casualty to be delivered to him still in their fantastic green body armor; he desperately wanted to examine that suit. The body of the small woman at his feet was a disappointment.

"She doesn't look like a soldier," Ping commented to Liang. "Did your men kill a clerk?"

The lieutenant's face dropped, "She isn't dead, Major." He nudged the body with his boot to prove the point. A low grunt followed from the presumed corpse. Despite the blood dripping from the gunshot wound in her left side, the woman was alive.

The expression on Ping's face slowly transformed to a harsh grin. "Get a medic up here at once." He clapped Liang's shoulder heartily, "Well done, Lieutenant. We now have a hostage!"

Zhongshan Park, Shanghai, PRC
2048APR21 09:15 CST (2048APR21 01:15 UTC)

Captain Yang watched, transfixed, as the alien aircraft struggled in its slow descent to the ground. Apparently not slow enough, she realized, as the landing gear collapsed when the odd plane made contact with the soft green field, canting away from Yang's vantage point. Vapors, or perhaps smoke, wafted away from several rents in the broken craft.

The aircraft (spaceship?) was midway between her position and the black tower in the distance. Yang waited to see which troops would rush forward and capture the pilot and crew. Two minutes later she still waiting when burning wreckage of other aircraft began to drop from the sky, leaving columns of smoke all around her as the wrecks landed on shops and other buildings along the park's perimeter.

Yang hesitated. This isn't how it was supposed to work; she was supposed to wait for orders from her superiors. But she knew she could not let the aliens escape simply because the colonel didn't have a working radio. She needed to act. Now!

She turned and pulled Wu Yenching from the line, "Go to detachment headquarters. Tell them we are securing the alien prisoners. Go!" She looked to Sergeant Bo, who nodded agreement before she set out across the field.

"First platoon, double-fast. On me," Bo shouted as he set out to catch up with his captain.

The soldiers closed on the downed spaceship, quickly surrounding it in a cautious ring thirty meters from the strange machine on all sides. Bo followed Yang as she swung to the far side of the wreckage, settling on what she presumed was some type of cockpit. She wasn't in the People's Liberation Army Air Force, but she had seen enough movies on TV to guess about the configuration.

She raised her pistol and stepped forward seven or eight meters, shouting in her strained English, "You are surround. Come out. Hands up!" Xiwang waited what she thought was an appropriate amount of time and was ready to repeat her instructions when movement stopped her.

With an audible hiss, the spacecraft canopy popped up a few centimeters, then slid forward with a hiss. This revealed a figure in red as it struggled to rise from the wreckage. The pilot, she assumed, was dressed in an odd mixture of a spacesuit like the ones the taikonauts wore years ago and the kind of flight-suit PLAAF pilots always wore in the recruiting posters Yang routinely saw around the city. The captain kept her gun trained on the alien as it stepped clear of its craft, jumping down onto the nearby grass.

When the alien's hands went up to grasp its helmet, Yang nearly shot it. "Hold your fire," she yelled to her people, cursing that she hadn't thought to say that earlier.

With some manipulation, the alien lifted the helmet away to reveal a very European face. "I am Flight Ensign Seweryn," he announced in vaguely Russian-accented English.

"Ensign Swerin," Yang struggled to repeat the name, "discard your weapon!"

"I have no weapon," the ensign returned. "No pistol," he corrected, glancing at his broken fighter.

Yang relaxed slightly, "You are under arrest, Ensign. Raise hands."

Seweryn tossed his helmet to the ground and slowly raised his arms in compliance. "Arrest? What are the charges?"

While four of her men surged forward and placed the pilot in restraints, Captain Yang holstered her pistol. "Not authorized landing," she explained with the hint of a smirk.

LT Chu watched all this unfold from her position behind the cordon, cheering to herself as she watched one after another Chinese aircraft drop from the sky. Then, silently cursing as she watched the nearby troops drag a Commonwealth pilot back from his crashed fighter. *At least the Chinese pilots won't be walking away from* their *landings*, she thought with morbid satisfaction.

She wanted to rush forward and grab a weapon from the nearest soldier, thinking she could take at least of few of them by surprise and free the pilot. But despite that desire, she knew better. At best, she could take out five or six of the enemy before they killed her. And most likely, the pilot would also perish in the crossfire. And for what? A small taste of revenge?

Instead, Chu stared in silence as smoke rose from several points near the midpoint of the Commonwealth tower. *As long as I'm free, I can still find a way to help them*, she repeated in her head. *I'm no good to them dead or captured.* She pulled her baseball cap lower and melted into the growing crowd.

CHAPTER 8

Terra Station, Terra orbit
2048APR21 01:24 UTC

"Report!" the Regent bellowed as he strode into the vast operations center of the Commonwealth's primary orbital facility. He waved off junior officers once he spotted his quarry.

"I believe that is my line," RADM Derbez commented, breaking from the officers huddled around a large circular display table.

"Always steal from the best," the Regent returned as he stepped up to the table. Peering down at the map projected across the table's surface. He directed his next demand at VADM Fitzpatrick, "What do we have?"

"The two fighters we launched from East Asia monitor were attacked," Erin began. She touched a control and colored indicators were added to the map. "Six fixed-wing and four rotary aircraft. They had some sophisticated weapons – both of our *Darts* were damaged. One is returning to the monitor; the other was forced to make an emergency landing near the office." She stared down at the two flashing blue icons, then touched a control to remove the ten red symbols. "All Chinese aircraft were destroyed."

"Alleged Chinese aircraft," CDRE Bombe corrected in his deep bass voice. "From the visuals we received, they had no markings."

The director of defense shook her head, "I don't care if they had 'Rebel Alliance' painted on their sides," Jiang declared in sarcasm she obviously picked up from the Regent over the years. "Those were products of China's aerospace industry; the configurations match their most recent models. There can be no doubt as to the identity of our attackers." She looked from Bombe to the Regent. "I cannot explain their weapons, but I know who threatens us."

The Regent nodded, then tossed out his next question to the group, "What *do* we know about their weapons?"

"Not much," Fitzpatrick admitted. "Possibly a high-velocity cannon; more likely some form of electromagnetic rail gun. We'll know more when the damaged fighter returns to its station, and we are able to examine it in detail."

"So, we have no fighters in the area now? We're blind?" the Regent questioned.

"No, sir," Bombe assured the leader of the Commonwealth. "We have two F-2's from Australia in the area, with two F-1's inbound from Monitor East Asia. The reinforcements will be onsite in three minutes."

The Regent followed this with the one question that stood foremost in his mind. "And when do the shuttles go in?"

Fitzpatrick exhaled slightly before answering, "We are re-equipping Captain Bruttius and his platoon. Their armor and heavy weapons were left behind when they travelled to Australia."

"Why wait? Why not use the troops already in Australia?" the Regent demanded.

"Bruttius' Sentries are the best choice; they know the layout of their office," MGEN Graham stated flatly. She looked to the Regent to see if he would challenge that statement, "We will add a platoon of Rangers to assist him, but our best chance of success comes with someone who knows the terrain."

The Regent nodded slowly. "OK. And when do they arrive? When does the rescue begin?" his voice rising as his frustration grew. He wanted answers, not handling!

Erin Fitzpatrick threw herself between the Regent's growing anger and the others around the table. "There is another problem. The fighters reported a … field. Interference below nine hundred meters that disrupted communications, sensors … even flight controls. We can't send in anyone until we can determine what is causing it and eliminate the threat." She paused, looking at the frustration evident in the Regent's face. "We can't risk a landing on the roof; a crash could kill people on the shuttlecraft *and* in the building."

"Land them further out," the Regent declared. "Away from the building."

"And what?" Graham demanded, not willing to tiptoe around their leader. "March through the city? Fight their way through the Chinese lines?" She shook her head, "We can't invade China with fifty people."

"You're not invading China!" the Regent shouted back. "You're rescuing our people. Don't send fifty; send them all. Everyone we have in Australia!"

Standing beside him, Jiang placed her hand on the Regent's. "Sir, we cannot declare war on China. You noted yourself, she is a part of the Commonwealth."

The Regent was ready to scream in the director's face but stopped himself when he met her eyes. *She's right.* He looked around the table. *And Argenta would be furious at how I have behaved. I can't keep doing this.* He was reverting to the inexperienced amateur he had been when the Ssenn first kidnapped him. He had to get control of himself; he had to remember who he was. "You're right," he agreed softly. "I'm sorry. I've been under a lot of pressure."

"Of course," Jiang agreed. "We understand."

"I'd appreciate it if no one mentioned this to … the former executive director when she returns," he explained, stumbling to avoid saying her name, lest it set him off again.

"That file's getting a might full, sir," Fitzpatrick chided the Regent with a wink.

The Regent smiled at his old protégé. "Then I guess we'll need a larger file, Admiral. Maybe a whole new cabinet."

"Yes, sir. I'll have the boys start on it right away," Erin agreed. "Orders, sir?"

The Regent looked down on the situation table as two new blue icons appeared. "As you have reminded me on many occasions, Admiral, I'm not allowed to give orders. I can only make suggestions." He looked around at the expectant faces, "I suggest you find a solution, and get our people home." With a nod, he turned and walked to the exit.

"Yes, sir," Fitzpatrick replied to his back.

Commonwealth Office (level 19), Shanghai, PRC
2048APR21 09:38 CST (2048APR21 01:38 UTC)

"Fall back," CPL Saputra yelled to the two Sentries still in the main corridor. They had been able to contain the Chinese forces until the enemy brought up one of their railguns; on each level, that was the sign to fall back to the next level. PVT1 Harper was already behind the corporal, securing the lift that was their escape pod. But Ngaporo and Klavina were still at least ten meters from the corridor junction. "Move faster!"

Just then a bolt from the Chinese railgun struck Klavina in the upper right arm, piercing her armor and causing her to lose her grip on her weapon. The private let loose a stream of profanity in her native language as she fell to the floor. Ngaporo saw this and stopped, crouching in a shooting stance rather than abandon Klavina.

"Damn it," Saputra growled as he moved to recover his teammate. "Ngaporo, cover me." He scrambled forward while keeping low, firing his weapon indiscriminately in the hope of forcing the Chinese marksman to seek cover rather than finish off his fallen comrade. Hooking his left arm under Klavina's uninjured shoulder, he forced her to her feet and the pair backpedaled to relative safety. "Let's go, Ngaporo!" the corporal called out.

Ngaporo rose up just enough to resume his retreat when a second bolt from the railgun pierced his faceplate, stopping halfway through the back of his helmet. The big Maori private stretched out and collapsed to the ground like a tree felled in the forest. He never uttered a word.

Saputra stopped in his tracks, stunned. Only the pinging of several bullets off his armor brought him back to his current circumstances. He dragged Klavina another twenty meters to the waiting lift, tossing her inside before collapsing in himself. "Go!" he ordered Harper.

"Where's Ngaporo?" Harper demanded, confused.

"GO!" Saputra shouted again. He was relieved when Harper complied, and the doors closed. While the lift car ascended to the next level, CPL Saputra slammed the back of his helmet against the lift wall in utter frustration.

When SSGT Mackenzie received the latest situation report, she said nothing, just gritted her teeth. Even after ten of her Sentries had been injured by the PLA's latest weapon, she never thought it would come to this. Private Ngaporo was her first casualty, and it didn't sit well. She ignored the dozens of enemy soldiers her people had cut down as they defended the office building – they were the aggressors, after all. They could all go to hell. *They attacked us! We are the ones with superior weapons; we have superior protection. Just not superior enough*, she was forced to admit.

"Where is he now?" she finally asked.

Saputra hesitated, then reluctantly admitted, "Still on nineteen."

Mackenzie was furious, shouting over the comms, "You left him?"

"I had no choice! I had to get Klavina out of there," Saputra fired back. "Would two dead have been better? Or three?"

Mackenzie recognized the mixture of emotions in the corporal's voice, the rage and the shame. It finally dawned on her that Saputra was the witness; he was right there as a teammate died under his watch. "No. You did the right thing. Is Klavina on twenty-eight?" After losing level fifteen, the Commonwealth forces had to relocate the infirmary to the Regent's guest quarters on twenty-eight. Mackenzie didn't think the Regent would mind. And if he did, he could always fire her.

"Yes, she's with Doctor Zhao now. Klavina's out of the fight," Saputra confirmed. "I'm heading back to twenty with Harper." The rage was gone from his voice, replaced by a cold anger that Mackenzie could understand. Unfortunately, it was the kind of anger that could quickly morph from resolve into the need for revenge. If she didn't want Franklin bravado before, she certainly didn't want a team bent on vendetta.

"Negative. I need you to get to twenty-two. Find Agent Wilson and combine with her team. You're in charge," the sergeant instructed. Two of the Commonwealth Security agents along with ENS Barzini and two Base security guards had found Sentry armor they could squeeze into (or in some cases was not too bulky to move around in). Unfortunately, none of the five had any combat experience. The closest they came was Agent Wilson, who had trained the with US Marines before joining Commonwealth Security. Thankfully, Barzini agreed with Mackenzie that Wilson should take charge of the 5-person team.

"Understood," Saputra agreed less than enthusiastically, fearing he was now demoted to babysitting duty with the ersatz fireteam. He closed the comms channel before Mackenzie could change her mind and assign him to guard the valuables in the Regent's quarters on twenty-nine.

In the brief moment of silence that followed, Mackenzie considered Wilson and her former service with the American Marines. Heather had studied the various ground forces of the homeworld, hoping to learn from their centuries of experience. *Maybe we need to adopt their standard*, she thought. *No man left behind.* Didn't the possibility of a Guardian killed in action ever occur to her superiors? Did they really think our armor was impervious? Mackenzie checked herself, realizing that until a few minutes ago, she had thought that very thing. *Yes*, she considered. *I really need to recommend that.*

With a heavy sigh, she mumbled, "Back to work."

Ping looked down into the lifeless eyes of Captain Xu, the high-tech plates in the combat vest he wore ineffective against the alien weapons as evidenced by the charred scar that passed through his spine and heart. Ping hoped his old friend died quickly, but feared it was not so.

The major stood and looked around as if seeing for the first time the countless bodies filling the hallway, in some places two or three deep. Somehow, he had blocked out the level of carnage here and in the stairwell. It was only when he spotted such a familiar face that he grasped the level of destruction the enemy had wrought. The earlier casualties on the tenth and fifteenth floors had been bad, but in those cases the wounded always outnumbered the dead. Here the numbers were reversed, as if the aliens had found some hidden reserve of determination as they realized they were running of out floors to which they could retreat, and so decided to slaughter his men rather than risk surrender.

For the first time Ping Youxia questioned his orders. Questioned if all this was worth the fleeting chance that the state could negotiate better terms with the humans from the stars. Was he really fighting for his country's liberation, or just a payoff for the fat old men in charge? He hung his head in disgust, first at the thought that it could be true, then at himself for letting doubt creep into his mind. He needed to be strong, for his men but also for China.

Ping spotted what remained of a railgun on its tripod; even at this distance he could tell the barrel was destroyed. No doubt, the operator was one of the bodies nearby. *Damn!* With this loss, they were down to three of the superweapons, though how *super* these guns were was now in question.

He noticed Liang standing a few meters further down the corridor. With Xu dead, Ping would normally turn to Captain Ho as next in line of command, but Ho died earlier on the fifteenth floor and Captain Kuo was lost here on the twentieth on the other side of the building. That left Ping with just two lieutenants, Liang being the senior. Even Ma was dead.

"Where is it?" Ping demanded of his new adjutant.

Liang stood a little taller with his new responsibilities, "This way, sir." He led Ping another dozen meters down the corridor to a huddle of soldiers staring down at the ground. "Make way," Liang bellowed.

Ping stepped forward and spotted the object of the soldier's curiosity. There on the floor lay the first alien armored soldier his troops could claim as a kill. Ping ignored the charred contents of the blackened helmet, focusing instead on the dark green armor that covered the chest and appendages. It was so unlike the vests he and his troops wore; the alien seemed encased with even armored gauntlets and boots, looking more like a green stormtrooper from a science fiction film than a real soldier. But Ping had to remind himself, they were real soldiers – soldiers who really killed over one hundred of his men. Their amazing weapons and this suit made that possible. *And now we have both.*

He snatched the alien's fallen weapon, finding it surprisingly light compared to the Type 44 assault carbine he normally carried. Waving his men to the side, he aimed the weapon at a wall while being careful not to bring it to shoulder level, just in case the recoil was such that it required an armored shoulder to compensate. He pulled on what had to be the trigger repeatedly with no effect. Holding the weapon closer to his eyes, he searched for a safety latch or mechanism, but could find none. Perhaps the ammunition was depleted, he reasoned. Or perhaps the weapon was somehow tied to the owner's gloved hand. They would need to experiment.

He handed the gun to Liang, then pointed at the body, "Get these to Sergeant Wu. I need to know how they work." A plan started to formulate. "Find a way to get that open without damaging it further."

Terra Monitor East Asia, Terra orbit
2048APR21 01:43 UTC

"It did what?" VADM Fitzpatrick's voice demanded. On the display, she stood beside CDRE Bombe, both of them on Terra Station.

"According to the ground crew, the pulse gun on Falcon-Four malfunctioned when the leading twelve centimeters of the crystal fractured," Ortiz explained.

Bombe shook his head, "How? Did the Chinese fighters do this with their cannons?"

"We don't think so, Commodore," Ortiz replied. "Their conventional shells could not produce the velocities needed. There was also a considerable amount of iron embedded in the debris. The weapons team think it is more likely that they used an electromagnetic cannon to produce the necessary force."

"Incredible," Fitzpatrick admitted, then wondered why she used that word. Earth military had been working with those types of weapons long before the arrival of the Commonwealth. Admittedly, those had been mounted on warships. Was shrinking the weapon down to a fighter jet really that surprising an achievement in almost thirty years? "Does this endanger all of the fighters?"

The commodore again shook his head, "The F-2's are shielded around the pulse gun; they should not have a problem. But we could hold the older *Darts* in reserve."

"We already launched a pair of F-1's to replace the wounded flight," CDR Jefferson reminded the group. "Do we recall them?"

Fitzpatrick considered the option for a moment. "Not at this time," she decided. "But keep them above one thousand." This led her to the next topic, "Where do we stand with the interference?"

Jefferson could sense Ortiz's relief that she was now out of the spotlight. The Base commander took over, "Let me check the latest." She turned to Duong, "Lieutenant, any improvement?"

Duong rose from his station, nudging PO1 Ruiz to do the same. The lieutenant addressed his response to the captain and the senior officers on the screen, "Not really. We still cannot pinpoint the source of the problem. It doesn't help that almost every Chinese satellite in orbit below us seems to be cycling through their EM spectrum. It's playing hell with our comms to the pilots, and just dumping noise our sensors have to filter out."

"Do we think they're doing this deliberately? A form of attack?" Fitzpatrick inquired.

With the commander and lieutenant looking directly at her, Ruiz felt compelled to provide the answer, "We've never seen this type of activity before, ma'am. Not over several years that I've been here. It seems like an unlikely coincidence."

"Yes," Erin agreed. "Yes, it does." She stood silent for several breaths before declaring, "I think we can find a work around." She turned her attention back to Jefferson, "Thank you for the update, Commander. We'll talk soon." The comms window disappeared from the main display without further warning.

Duong looked from the display to Jefferson and Ortiz. "So that's it? We just wait?"

Jefferson nodded in sympathy, "Yes, Lieutenant. What else is new." She folded her arms, "We wait."

CHAPTER 9

White House, Washington, DC, USA
2048APR20 21:57 EDT (2048APR21 01:57 UTC)

Lucian Scott-Marshall descended the stairs to the White House Situation Room in a sweatshirt and jeans, albeit a sweatshirt emblazoned with the seal of the President of the United States. Lucian believed his workday ended two hours earlier when he retired to the residence, but apparently, he'd been mistaken. The White House Chief of Staff greeted him just outside the situation room door.

"I am sorry, Mr. President, but there is an incident we need to address," Marcia Lynch informed him softly as he reached her.

Seeing the look of concern on Lynch's face, the president pressed her, "What is it? An earthquake? Natural disaster or something man-made?" He stopped, "Don't tell me it's another shooting?"

Lynch opened the door, urging the president to step inside. With the door closed behind them, she answered, "International."

Scott-Marshall missed a step, then corrected his action. *International?* The United States hadn't faced an international incident in over twenty years. Only the second African-American to reach the highest office in the land, Lucian had no illusions that he wielded the same power as his predecessor, even given the man's short tenure. The former policeman of the world was enjoying a retirement forced upon the United States by the Solar Commonwealth. President Scott-Marshall's power largely ended at the nation's borders.

"We're not able to connect the vice president at this time," Lynch continued. With reelection coming up, Lucian's running mate was in Los Angeles attending a fundraiser. "We'll update her once she returns to Air Force Two."

Stepping into the situation room proper, the president found his national security team already assembled. On one side of the table Annabelle Clark, the National Security Adviser, sat next to Secretary of Defense Perry. Lynch took her seat opposite Clark, while Secretary of State Benitez sat opposite Perry. At the head of the table, Lucian sat between the two senior advisors, "Ladies, gentleman. What precisely is the issue?"

"Mr. President, there is some unusual activity going on in Shanghai," Clark announced, diving right in.

Scott-Marshall suppressed a grin, "This isn't the good-old days. There really isn't all that much that we can do about activities in China." He looked from side to side for confirmation of his snap assessment. "Whatever it is, it is a problem for the Commonwealth."

"That's just it, sir," Lynch countered. "The problem seems to be between the Chinese and the Commonwealth."

"What?" the president blurted out.

Roger Perry spoke up, "General Bronson can explain."

The president finally noticed the tall officer in Air Force blue standing by the room's massive computer monitor. "Where's General Hammond?" he asked.

Again, Perry jumped in, "If you recall, the Chairman is currently in Vancouver, meeting with his Canadian counterpart."

The president nodded. The United States was still trying to reestablish better relations with its neighbor to the north as well as with Australia, citing long-held ties and common cultures. The task was complicated by the fact that those two nations apparently enjoyed privileged status with the Commonwealth thanks to their early recognition. While economic ties were largely welcomed between the three countries, America's former partners saw little need for military cooperation. "Yes … right," Lucian agreed. Waving to Bronson, "Please continue."

LGEN Bronson nodded and activated the monitor to show a wide-angle image of the western area of Shanghai, from the river on the east to the city's downtown airport in the west. "Three hours ago, Shanghai suffered a massive power failure, affecting most of the old city on the western side of the river." Clicking a control, the image zoomed in slightly as red icons began to appear. "Almost immediately, military forces began to take up key positions around the city."

"Is that unusual?" the president asked, looking to Perry. "Wouldn't we do the same if Los Angeles or Houston suddenly went dark?"

The SecDef smiled, "We would, but we'd never get so many troops deployed so quickly. And neither could China last August. When

Shenzhen lost power, it took them two hours to get troops out to sites not adjacent to their barracks, and nearly six hours to regain control of traffic."

"So? They learned from their mistakes," Rosalinda Benitez suggested.

Perry shook his head, "To deploy that many troops that quickly, they had to know when that blackout would occur, hours in advance." He looked to Bronson, "Show them."

The general clicked his control again and the image leaped forward until it focused on a smaller area centered on a large greenspace surrounded by urban sprawl. The president marveled at the clarity of the image. America may have lost most of her navy and all her overseas bases, but she maintained the most advanced network of surveillance satellites on the planet. If you didn't include the Commonwealth.

One thing in the image did strike the president as odd – the complete absence of traffic. He would have expected a tangle of cars and buses clogging every surface road and highway in the area. Hell, he would have expected that even without the blackout. Instead, all the roads were clear. "Where is everybody?" he asked.

"Precisely, Mr. President," Perry confirmed. "If this were any other city in the world … any other city in China, there would be masses of people and vehicles stranded in the chaos. That's precisely why we deploy troops. To reestablish order." He gestured to the screen. "Where is the disorder?"

"Actually, Mr. President, the real focus of this image is the building at the center," Bronson informed the group. He highlighted the location in question in gold. "That is the Commonwealth building in Shanghai," he declared. Another highlight formed a red ring some distance around the building, "And that is a full regiment of troops surrounding it."

Again, the detail of the image was impressive, revealing the military vehicles and groups of soldiers forming the perimeter. "They could be there to prevent looters from reaching the building. But there are no signs of looters anywhere in the city," Perry commented. "Or they could be there to make sure no one leaves the building."

"It should be noted, the Regent is reportedly living there at the moment," Clark added.

Scott-Marshall turned to look at his national security adviser and secretary of defense, weighing the implications. "Are you suggesting the Chinese are trying to contain the Regent?" he asked, then moved that idea to the next level, "That they are trying to capture him?" He looked around the table, "Is that even possible?"

Lynch shook her head. "I wouldn't have thought so," she began. "But can we afford to ignore the possibility?"

The president sat stunned, as Bronson continued. "There has also been increased activity by the Commonwealth, primarily their new base in Australia and their battle station over Asia." A new image replaced the eerily quiet image of the area, now with plumes of smoke rising from several locations. "Thirty minutes ago, we detected evidence of air combat over the area. At least one of the downed aircraft bears Commonwealth markings."

"This is incredible," was all the president could say in response. The idea of any nation on Earth challenging the mighty Commonwealth seemed insane. How could they do it? How could they risk the retaliation? "How will all this affect us?"

Clark again took the lead, "Sir, we have to consider the possibility that the Chinese could succeed. That could radically alter the power structure across the globe."

The president was still wrapping his mind around this concept, "Define success. Are they going to take control of the Commonwealth? Replace it somehow?"

"They could use this situation to negotiate improved terms for their country," Clark offered. "Recall, our two nations were the last to recognize the Commonwealth's claims. Any improvement China may receive would likely come at our expense."

Lynch chimed in, "It is also possible that this could topple the current leadership. China may already have an ally within the Commonwealth. There may be an agreement outlining what China will receive in exchange for assisting this person's rise to power."

"Sir, I know all this sounds crazy," the secretary of state confirmed. "But the Chinese make long-term plans. If they truly are behind this, then they know how it will benefit them, even if we can't see it yet."

"And what do you suggest we do about all this?" Scott-Marshall demanded.

Annabelle Clark eyed the others around the table before commenting, "There is the Commonwealth office in New York …" She let the idea hang in the air.

The president was wide-eyed, "Are you suggesting we do the same thing? You want to try to capture the other office? You just told me the Regent is in Shanghai! There's no one of comparable value in New York." He studied Clark and Perry, who did not seem deterred. "The Chinese must have been planning this for months. Years even. We can't just whip together an attack on the most powerful force on the planet, in the middle of our largest city, in an hour. That guarantees disaster."

At the end of the table, Bronson commented, "There is Operation Restored Freedom. That plan could be implemented on your order."

"Sir, we're not suggesting taking hostages. Simply a demonstration that we will not allow China to have unequal influence over the Commonwealth." He gestured across the table to Benitez, "If this does result in a power vacuum within the Commonwealth hierarchy, there may be other contenders for the throne who will be looking for allies."

Lucian looked around the table at the earnest faces. People he had known for years; people whose opinion he trusted. And they were suggesting madness; a suicide pact that would lead to the destruction of the country he swore to protect.

"Sir, we could review the plan. Perhaps make modifications if you are concern …" Marcia Lynch began but the president cut her off.

"Enough!" he announced, slapping the tabletop with a thunderous hand. "Not another word, is that clear?" His gaze scanned the table, staring down any dissent. He turned to Bronson, "General, I want every physical copy of that report rounded up and destroyed. Every electronic copy erased. No trace that it ever existed. Anyone who worked on it … I want them buried. Sent to the most remote base we still have. Alaska, Guam … wherever. We can't let the Commonwealth find out we ever remotely considered this."

"Sir," Clark began.

"No," Lucian cut her off. Standing, he looked down on the people around the table. "I don't know what the hell the Chinese were thinking. As a Christian, I can only pray that God shows them mercy." He turned towards the door, "Because I guarantee the Regent won't!"

CSS Bavaria, Terra orbit
2048APR21 02:08 UTC

LCDR Valiukaite looked up from her display, "Approaching position, Captain."

"Thank you, XO," CAPT Caoimhin Cinnéidigh replied. He hesitated only a moment before ordering, "Helm, reduce speed. Take us in."

"Aye, aye, sir," the young Somali officer answered from her station. Gliding her hands along the surface of her controls, she slowed the light cruiser while bringing the bow down. The image on the main display added a scarlet glow as the ship's vibration changed. "Down thirty degrees," LTJG Warsame confirmed.

Caoimhin sighed. *Bavaria* was a new ship, having launched only the previous year. Which was one reason she was available for this assignment – they had been in orbit of the homeworld taking on supplies. The captain disliked the thought of what this maneuver would do to the balance of their StarDrive nacelles; starships were not designed to enter the atmosphere. But like it or not, those were his orders.

"Altitude seven-zero kay-em; approaching longitude one-four-zero," the pilot informed the bridge.

"Shields?" the captain asked of the executive officer.

"Survived," Valiukaite responded.

Cinnéidigh looked at the XO with irritation, "That's not funny, Gabija."

The XO suppressed her smile, "Sorry, sir. Shields holding; pressure within tolerances."

"Better," Caoimhin answered back, not nearly as annoyed with his long-time friend as his expression indicated. *Bavaria* was a new command, and Cinnéidigh was determined not to fall into the lax patterns that developed when they served together on the *Osaka*.

"Approaching three-two kay-em; speed Mach 5. Leveling off," the helmsperson announced.

"Sensors?" the captain prompted.

From his station behind Valiukaite, the senior sensor officer answered, "Active and recording, Captain."

"Approaching coastline," Warsame informed the group. Turning her head to glimpse the captain over her right shoulder, "Captain, how are the Chinese going to react to this?"

"The shields aren't there just to protect us from friction, Lieutenant," Cinnéidigh reminded her. "Reduce speed to Mach 3."

"Aye, sir," Warsame returned. "Now entering Chinese airspace."

"Readings look good," LT Quiacala followed from the sensor station.

"Area is clear," Valiukaite added. To the captain, this was the most critical information.

A tense two minutes followed as Quiacala completed his task. The silence was broken when Warsame announced, "Exiting designated area."

Turning his chair to face the sensor station, the captain asked, "Did you get what we came for, Lieutenant? Or do we need to make another pass?"

Checking his console, their Mayan sensor officer looked apologetic, "A second pass would be helpful, sir. Just to be certain."

Cinnéidigh turned forward again, "You heard the man, Miss Warsame. Come about, reciprocal course." He raised an eyebrow to the XO, who shrugged in return.

"Coming about," the helmsperson replied. On the display the image swept as the ship completed its turn to port, then steadied. "On course."

"Sensors recording," Quiacala reported.

Only twenty seconds in, Valiukaite broke the silence, "Captain, we've piqued someone's interest. Two … correction three interceptors rising."

"Can they catch us?" Caoimhin asked.

The XO shook her head, "No. But their missiles might."

Cinnéidigh considered that, then dismissed the possibility. "Maintain course and speed."

Another minute followed before Warsame announced, "Coming up on the coast."

The captain released the tension in his shoulders. "Mister Quiacala, I hope you got everything you needed."

"Yes, sir," the sensor officer answered. "Thank you, Captain."

Cinnéidigh smiled softly, "Helm, take us back into space." He turned to his left to face the officer at the comms station, "Ensign, transmit all data to Terra Station once we clear the atmosphere."

Caoimhin hoped that the analysts at Terra Station were as satisfied with their results as Quiacala seemed. Otherwise, *Bavaria* would have to do this all over again.

Commonwealth Office (level 25), Shanghai, PRC
2048APR21 10:11 CST (2048APR21 02:11 UTC)

Argenta Quintilius was reaching the end of her patience. After hours of waiting in the pantry of her suite on the top level, away from any windows, she gave in to her frustration and descended to the guest level to find it converted into a hospital.

After living a lifetime in the clean, orderly city of Nova Roma and later in the various facilities of the Commonwealth, she was not accustomed to the pain and suffering she found there. Over a dozen Sentries and security guards in various degrees of discomfort filled a large dining area converted into a makeshift hospital ward, all under the care of the office's one doctor. But the worst was knowing that the numbers were going to increase very soon.

Down two more levels, she walked into the conference room, noting the new arrangement of tables meant to mimic the old operations office. Scanning the room, she located her target. "Lieutenant Hale?"

Hale stopped his discussion in mid-sentence and turned towards the sound of his name. "Madame Consort."

Quintilius' eyes grew cold, "Do not call me that, young man."

Hale froze in place. "My apologies … Director?" he offered, unsure as to what title he should use.

Argenta softened her expression, "Better." She looked around the room. "I assume there has been no progress in reaching Terra Station."

"No, ma'am," Hale confirmed. "But there has been Flight activity in the area, so we know that the monitor station is aware of the problem. I'm sure they are working on a solution." He tried to maintain a positive attitude when speaking with the civilians, hoping to avoid panic or worse.

"I observed the Flight activity – at least one of the craft was damaged and forced to land. Were you able to rescue the pilot?" Quintilius asked plainly.

Hale's eyes flicked away and down, wishing that the former executive director of the Commonwealth was less observant. This was only complicating his already difficult job, "No. We were already cut off from the exits at that time. Even if we weren't, the building is sealed tight during lockdown; we can't get outside."

Argenta gave Hale a cold stare for a second. "And yet, our attackers have no trouble entering the building." She saw Hale look away again. "I am not blaming you Lieutenant, nor am I suggesting anyone is derelict in their duties. I am simply assessing our situation."

"Yes, ma'am," the lieutenant commented. "Now, if you'll return to your residence …"

"I see little value in cowering in the Regent's quarters," Argenta replied as she began to examine the room, hoping to gain new insight into their situation.

Perhaps it was the culmination of the past few hours of stress, but Jonathan Hale decided to push back. "Ma'am, we have a job to do, and your presence doesn't make that easier. I need you to return to the Regent's quarters." When she continued to watch him in silence, he added with a bit more fervor, "Now."

"And if I refuse?" Quintilius asked politely. "I am not under your command, Lieutenant. I'm not even in the government anymore."

"Until Commander Hirsch returns, I am in charge of this facility. And anyone in this facility, for whatever reason, is subject to my orders," Hale explained coldly. "If you refuse to follow instructions, I will have Petty Officer Velasquez escort you to your quarters. He can carry you, if necessary."

Quintilius managed to suppress a smile at the young lieutenant's sudden surge of authority. Recognizing that a direct challenge of that authority was inappropriate, she altered her tactics. "What do they want?"

The change disoriented Hale, "Want? Who?"

"The invaders. What do they want?" Argenta repeated.

"We don't know. They haven't communicated with us," Hale explained. "We assume they mean to capture this facility, most probably with the goal of securing your group of VIPs. If they arrived a few hours earlier, they could have captured the Regent."

This aligned with Argenta's own thoughts. "A reasonable assumption. Following that line of reasoning, if we give them what they seek, the need for fighting ends."

"Give them what they seek?" Hale repeated, attempting to define just what the former director was suggesting. "You want us to surrender?" he demanded in shock.

"Not us. Me," Quintilius corrected Hale. "I have no desire to endanger the rest of the Regent's staff, nor any of your people or the Sentries. And as we have already established, I am not a member of the government. Still, in the absence of the Regent, I believe I am the next most valuable hostage, as it were."

"No," Hale stated flatly.

"It is a reasonable course of action," Quintilius continued. "Lacking the prospect of rescue, ending the fighting must be our priority."

"No," Hale repeated.

"Lieutenant, I have no desire to see more of our people injured or killed. If this one action can prevent it, then we should do it. It is a reasonable solution."

"No," Hale declared a third time, shaking his head to be certain that the older woman got the message. "We're not doing that. Is that clear? Not. Doing. That." He looked about the room, "All these people understand that. Why can't you?"

"Lieutenant, be reasonable," Argenta cajoled.

"Reasonable?" Hale's voice rose up, causing others in the room to turn their heads. "Reasonable? Madame Quintilius, I'd rather face the entire Chinese army than the Regent's wrath for going along with this scheme. At least I'm allowed to shoot back at the Chinese."

"We should discuss this with the senior Sentry," Quintilius continued.

Hale was emphatic, "We're not discussing this further. Not with anyone."

"Sir," PO2 Peraza called over to Hale from the comms station. "We have contact. They wish to speak with you."

"Terra Station?" Hale demanded as he moved to stand next to the petty officer.

"No, sir. Internal," Peraza explained. "I think it's the Chinese."
Hale stopped dead, looking back to Quintilius, who raised an eyebrow.

JOHN LALLIER

CHAPTER IO

Commonwealth Office (level 20), Shanghai, PRC
2048APR21 10:13 CST (2048APR21 02:13 UTC)

Ping looked at the wall-mounted device next to the elevator doors, repeating in English, "I will speak with your command officer." His original attempt to make himself understood in Mandarin had proven ineffective. *Typical*, he growled in frustration. *They come to our land and expect* us *to learn* their *language.*

"Standby," the voice from the speaker answered.

After a brief delay a new voice demanded, "Who is this?"

The major steeled himself and ignored the question, returning to his own, "You are command officer of building?"

"This is Lieutenant Hale; I am the current commanding officer of Solar Commonwealth Office Shanghai," the voice confirmed. "I ask again, to whom am I speaking?"

A mere lieutenant? Ping was not impressed. He had expected an officer of rank equal to his own. "I command forces below you. We control most of floors. Your time is over."

The line went dead for a moment. When it returned to life, a woman's voice appeared, "You have not identified yourself; are you PLA? Why are you here?"

Ping Youxia was surprised that the new voice spoke Chinese. Not only that, but the accent sounded like a local. He expected that the aliens would have one of their pet Chinese speak for them; they were able to form the words, but the accent was always very off. He didn't know which offended him more – an alien pet or a local who turned her back on her country. He decided the latter was worse. "I do not speak with traitors," he spat back.

Again, the line was muted, until the woman spoke again, "I am Wu Jing, Crewman, First Class. *I* am not the traitor here!" The words dripped with anger. "What do you wish to discuss?"

The traitorous mouse has grown a spine, he thought with amusement. *No matter.* "You are running out of time. Your capture is guaranteed." He paused to glance at the pad Private Long handed him. "We have already captured one of your fellows. Crewman Lindfors," he struggled with the pronunciation, "is our guest. She is unharmed and will remain so. If you cooperate."

This time the microphone stayed live, and Ping was able to hear a muted discussion in English. He was only able to make out a few of the words, but it seemed to him that the aliens were a less than united front.

The traitor returned, "Her continued wellbeing is your best guarantee of similar treatment when our forces capture you."

The waver in her voice told Ping she was not as confident as her words indicated. "Surrender now. And we will allow the civilians to live," Ping ordered.

"And our soldiers?" Wu asked.

Ping was disgusted by the traitor's question. "All invaders, all who would steal what is ours, will be punished."

A new voice answered – another woman, this one in awkward Chinese with a hint of the alien accent, "I plan to ask the Regent to be merciful. Now I do not." This time, when the line went dead the small light next to the speaker winked out.

Ping turned to Liang, "Resume the assault."

Quintilius' hand was still resting on the comms control. "I apologize. I allowed my emotions to act against my better judgement." She looked to Hale and CRW1 Wu, "I must be picking up bad habits from the Regent."

"Not at all, ma'am," Hale assured her. "I would have done the same, but you were closer to the button."

Argenta smiled weakly, "Thank you, Lieutenant. It appears you were correct: my surrender would not guarantee the survival of the rest of our people." She turned her attention to Wu, "Crewman, it grieves me that your countrymen would treat you so."

"You understood?" Wu blurted in surprise, bringing her hands to her mouth, then immediately returned them to her sides as she stood with her head higher, "Ma'am, it doesn't matter what he said. Not to me. I am proud to be here serving the Commonwealth. And you should know, many Chinese feel the same. There are some who think we were better off before … before you came. But they are not the majority. They do not speak for us!"

Quintilius nodded solemnly, "I am pleased to hear that, Miss Wu. Your dedication does you great credit. And I know the Regent would say the same. Only better … and certainly with more words." She grinned slightly.

"Thank you, ma'am," Wu beamed, then turned to her superior, "Lieutenant." She hurried back to her assigned station.

"She is too young. She doesn't remember a time before the Commonwealth," Argenta commented. "And neither do you, Lieutenant." She looked to make sure the officer was not offended by her observation. "But the two of you, and all the rest, are the reason the Commonwealth was created. You are our future." She gestured towards the comms control, "The petty arguments of our friend here are the past. Remember that. Their cruelty is the product of their fear; our compassion comes from knowing we are the future. Do what you must to protect that future, but only what you must do. I will not have retributions committed in the name of the Commonwealth."

"Yes, ma'am," the lieutenant readily agreed, then looked away as increased activity at two stations caught his eye. "If you'll excuse me," he mumbled as he moved away.

Quintilius nodded despite having no audience, then moved towards the exit. *Back upstairs,* she thought to herself sadly. *I really am picking up too many bad habits from him. I'm just glad he wasn't there to witness my speech. He'd feel compelled to offer pointers.*

People's Armed Police, Shanghai, PRC
2048APR21 10:15 CST (2048APR21 02:15 UTC)

Hirsch sat in the windowless room, counting the dots in a specific ceiling tile for the eighteenth time. At least he finally stopped checking his wrist for the time on his confiscated band. He couldn't be certain how long he had been left waiting. The captain who insisted on speaking with him was conveniently absent when he arrived at the police building with his escort. Rather than apologize for the confusion, his escort dumped into this room to await the captain's return. Whenever that might be.

A sound at the door caused his concentration to slip and he lost count. *Finally*, he thought. The door opened and a private stepped in, brandishing a rifle. He stepped to the table in front of Hirsch and glanced down menacingly. When it seemed the soldier was satisfied, he turned to the door and barked out a single word Hirsch did not recognize, then moved to stand in a nearby corner of the room.

A junior lieutenant entered next; she carefully placed an actual paper folder on the table, then stood aside as an older officer entered the room and the door closed behind him. The final visitor was somewhat portly and balding in his dark green uniform, clearly the leader of the group. He took the seat opposite Hirsch while the junior officer sat to his left and slightly away from the table.

The man pulled a pair of reading glasses from his jacket pocket, then made a show of opening the folder and reading the top page. At last, he spoke, "Hirsch, Albrecht. Lieutenant Commander." He looked up and studied Hirsch's eyes, "This is you?"

Hirsch tilted his head in dismay. "It is. And who are you?"

The man placed the still open folder on the table. "I am Colonel Cheng Jinrui, People's Armed Police, First Mobile Detachment, Shanghai."

"Very good to meet you, Colonel," Hirsch replied, deciding to leave out the 'at last' he was tempted to add. "Why am I here?"

Cheng's gaze returned to the folder, reviewing several more pages before closing the material. "Commander, why are you not in uniform?"

Hirsch tamped down the urge to snap back, instead pausing as Cheng had done previously. "I was off-duty when your men detained me. I don't know the regulations for your service, but we are not required to be in uniform at all times." Folding his arms, he pressed, "Now can I get an answer to my question?"

Cheng removed his reading glasses and placed them on the folder. "There have been a number of … events. In and around your residence. We would like some explanation."

Albrecht's confusion showed on his face. "You mean the Commonwealth tower? What type of events."

"There is a power outage, covering a sizeable area of the city, centered on your building. Military spacecraft arrived shortly after, firing weapons in the vicinity. And for some reason, radio communication is disrupted within a radius of four kilometers of the black tower," Cheng paused in his litany. "Can you explain any of this?"

Hirsch shook his head, "Colonel, I have been locked in this room for … well I can't tell you for how long since your men confiscated my band." He raised his left arm to reveal the unadorned wrist.

Cheng squinted, then looked to the lieutenant, who reached into her jacket pocket and extracted the item in question. She leaned forward and placed it in Albrecht's waiting hand. "We will continue to hold your mobile phone until your departure," Cheng declared.

Hirsch accepted the band, examining it before returning it to its usual location. "I have been here for over three hours. As far as I recall, there was no problem with the electricity near Jing'An Temple when your men accosted me. As for the aerospace craft, we don't have any assigned to the office. Have you contacted Terra Station about those?"

Cheng continued to study Hirsch's face, "As with you, space stations are outside my immediate area of authority." He leaned back, "Perhaps you can explain reports of weapons fire coming from within your building. I presume that would be within your assigned responsibilities."

Hirsch looked up sharply, leaning forward and drawing the attention of the armed guard. A raised hand from Cheng caused the man to lower his weapon. Albrecht ignored the threat. "I need to contact my office. Now!" He was tired of accommodating the locals.

Cheng shook his head, "As I said earlier, communication is disrupted within four kilometers of your building. That includes this facility." He softened his tone, perhaps to place the prisoner at ease, "We are forced to dispatch a mobile unit outside the affected area to make contact with Beijing."

"Then let me use that to contact Terra Station," Hirsch insisted.

"Of course, Commander," Cheng agreed. "Once I am satisfied that you are not involved in these events."

"Colonel, I don't have time for this," Hirsch barked. "I'm responsible for over one hundred people in that building, and you've just informed me that someone is shooting in there."

Cheng nodded, "I appreciate your concern for those hundred people." His smiled slipped, "We are concerned with the welfare of over twenty million citizens of this city." He allowed that comparison to hang in the air. "Now, explain to me again why you are out of uniform and away from your post when all this is occurring."

Hirsch recognized that this was going to take a while. Folding his arms, he leaned back in his seat and thought, *I just hope Hale has everything under control.*

Terra Station, Terra orbit
2048APR21 02:26 UTC

"Did we find something useful?" the Regent demanded as he walked up to the planning table in the operations center.

"Yes, sir," Fitzpatrick confirmed from her position in the center of the group. "The data from *Bavaria* was considerable, but I think we have what we were looking for." She tapped a control on the table to restore the earlier image of the area around the Shanghai office, this time zooming out a bit further to include surrounding districts of the city. A second touch highlighted a number of structures in yellow. "Despite the failure of the electrical grid, these buildings still show signs of power."

The Regent studied the map, finding no pattern in the distribution of buildings across this portion of the city. "What are they?"

"Some are hospitals or government buildings, the type we would expect to have emergency generators. Four are office blocks; two residential buildings," RADM Derbez explained. "Alone, this is not unusual given the importance of this city to the Chinese economy."

"This, however, is unusual," Fitzpatrick continued. Touching a control, a dull red haze settled across much of the display. "There is a wide pattern of EM emissions across this area, not only covering the frequencies used by local communications and information systems, but also bands reserved for the use of Commonwealth forces."

"And this is the interference that is blocking our signal to Shanghai, and why we can't land the shuttlecraft?" the Regent added.

"Yes. But the interesting part is this," VADM Fitzpatrick announced. Now the red haze became thin red lines, crossing and recrossing neighboring lines to form an enormous web. As the Regent focused on the lines, he began to see that these were not a collection of random straight lines, but instead concentric irregular rings, all radiating outward from five points of concentration. "This shows the distribution of the EM emissions at specific increments across the area. It increases to its highest level around these five structures." A further tweak of the display revealed increasingly thicker red lines forming five bullseyes.

The Regent nodded, "And what are those buildings."

Derbez answered again, "Two of the buildings belong to the country's two main telecom companies. One belongs to a large commercial bank; one is a government building." As the admiral spoke, each of the buildings received a numbered icon. Each of the buildings was now highlighted in bright red and yellow. With dramatic timing, Derbez finished, "And one is a residential tower currently under construction. Officially unoccupied."

The Regent looked around the faces at the table, waiting for one of them to explain why an unoccupied building was running emergency generators during a blackout. But of course, there was only one explanation – someone was using the building for their own purposes. A wave of anger built up in the Regent, "We have fighters in the area. If they take out these buildings, is our problem solved?"

"Sir?" MGEN Graham spoke with alarm. "When you say 'take out', what exactly do you mean?"

The Regent did not flinch, "I mean hit them with missiles. Destroy their generators or whatever broadcast equipment they have."

"Sir, the sensor data is not that detailed," Derbez explained. "We don't know where this equipment is in each building. It is likely any transmitter would be on one of the higher floors, while the generators would likely be on ground level if not in basements."

"We'd have to destroy the buildings to ensure success," Graham declared. "I'm not sure the fighters have that kind of ordnance." She looked to Fitzpatrick, "A ship in orbit would be able to do it."

"I'm not going to order *Bavaria* to open fire on a city," Fitzpatrick replied angrily, then looked down the table to the Regent. "Never!"

The Regent held up his hands in surrender, "I didn't suggest that."

"Sir," CDRE Bombe spoke up for the first time. "Do you recall the *Zhukov* incident?"

The Regent looked from Bombe to Fitzpatrick, "When the ship was damaged by the Korhvallan harvester?"

"No, sir. In 2019, when the *Zhukov* was damaged while in low orbit over the United States," Bombe explained.

Of course, the Regent realized. "It was 2020, actually. The EM pulse weapon."

Bombe smiled discreetly, "Yes, sir. We have developed a similar energy pulse missile. It should be possible to disable the generators and the transmitters with a single missile, assuming they are both within eight hundred meters when the warhead is triggered. To be certain, we could adjust the effective radius up to two kilometers."

"That would affect the office as well," Graham challenged.

"The office is shielded," Derbez countered. He looked to Fitzpatrick, "As I recall, that is what saved you and *Honshu* from a similar fate."

"Yes," Fitzpatrick nodded to Derbez, then turned to Bombe, "but the blast will also affect every other building in the area." She looked to the Regent, "We'd be cutting power to hospitals and other emergency services the people of this city need."

The Regent stared down at the map on the table display. "Where are the hospitals?" With a beep, an icon appeared over several of the yellow-highlighted buildings. One was directly across the street from the #4 red-shaded building; directly across from the government building if the Regent's memory served. Not good, he admitted until he noticed a second hospital further down that same road, well away from the government building or any of the other numbered buildings. "It looks like only one hospital could be affected, and they could evacuate people to that nearby hospital if needed."

"Sir," Fitzpatrick started.

"Acceptable risk, Admiral," the Regent declared, cutting off any argument. "We didn't start this, and I will do what we can to minimize the danger to the citizens of that city. But we also didn't install a transmitter so close to that hospital. I'm certainly not going to reward the people who did." He looked to Bombe, "Commodore, keep the effective range to the minimum needed to disable the jamming devices and their power sources. No more, but no less. How soon can we have your fighters in the area?"

Bombe looked to Fitzpatrick, who gave a curt nod. "Ten minutes to change out ordnance; thirty to be onsite."

"And the Sentries? How long to have them on the roof of the main building?" the Regent followed up.

Bombe consulted a tablet in front of him. "The launch isn't as fast as the fighters, but if we get it into the air while the fighters are arming, it will only be ten to twelve minutes behind. Which would give us time to establish if the pulse missiles are effective."

The Regent nodded. "Thank you all. Admiral, walk with me," he declared as he stepped from the table and turned towards the exit.

Fitzpatrick hurried to catch the Regent, reaching him when he was halfway to the doors, "Sir?"

The Regent stopped, then looked about to check that they were away from any other people. In a low voice, he announced, "Erin, I know I'm not supposed to give you orders, so I'm only going to say this one time." He took a deep breath, then in hushed tones finished, "Make it so."

CHAPTER II

Commonwealth Office (level 24), Shanghai, PRC
2048APR21 10:34 CST (2048APR21 02:34 UTC)

SSGT Mackenzie studied the readings on her faceplate. "Leekpai, fall back to the lifts. Now! No arguments!" Heather was getting pretty tired of her people making brave but ultimately futile stands. Earlier, two of her Sentries were trapped on level twenty-two when they failed to fall back to the lifts in time and the enemy breached both stairwells. To escape capture, they were forced to blow out a window in one of the offices and climb up cables dropped down from the roof. Even now, she had two Commonwealth Security sharpshooters stationed on the roof to pick off any enemy soldiers that attempted to follow their route up the side of the building. So far, the body count was five, and Mackenzie was more than ready to list those as KIA after a 68-meter fall to the courtyard below.

"On our way up, Sarge," CPL Leekpai acknowledged. "We have two more wounded, including Lieutenant Barzini." The corporal paused, lowering her voice slightly, "And Saman's body."

"Acknowledged," Mackenzie answered with a sigh. "Get them to the doctor on twenty-eight." She hated the idea that the wounded would have to climb the stairs from twenty-five to the field hospital on twenty-eight, but she needed the lift held at twenty-five to block the shaft. If not, they would have enemy soldiers behind their line, such as it was. It also pained her to lose another man, doubly so with CRW2 Saman since the man was Base security and not really trained for this. In Heather's mind, Saman died because her Sentries were understaffed. That made it her fault.

The sound of the cutting torch attacking the door to her right brought Mackenzie out of her guilt. "Creticus? Status?" she called out.

The voice of the Roman corporal leading the fire team in the other stairwell came back immediately. "They'll be through in less than two minutes, Sergeant."

"Fall back to twenty-six," Mackenzie instructed. With only a fire door to protect the stairwell on twenty-five, there was no point in trying to make a stand there. Thankfully, it was the last fire door in the building;

nothing but security doors to the higher levels. "I'll take my team down the corridor on twenty-five; maybe we can get some of the black hats to chase us."

"Understood, Sergeant. Up two," CPL Creticus answered. "Let me know when you want me to come down and save your ass."

Mackenzie chuckled at the Roman's confidence, then looked back to the Sentry and security person that made up her team. "Let's move. Up one and down the south corridor. Harper, lead us out. Lezhneva, stay between me and Harper." the sergeant ordered.

The crewperson in the blue Base uniform looked concerned. "Down the corridor, Sergeant?"

"Don't worry, Crewman. Just keep your fire on the bad guys. And when the bullets start flying, stick behind me or Harper. We are your shields," Heather tried to re-assure the only person not wearing armor. With a final glance at the torch's progress, "Let's go."

Commonwealth Office (level 23), Shanghai, PRC
2048APR21 10:38 CST (2048APR21 02:38 UTC)

Ping was leaning against a wall and resting his eyes when the voice interrupted his moment of peace. "Sir?"

He opened his eyes to find a corporal standing in front of him. He couldn't remember the man's name and the tag on his uniform was obscured by layers of dried blood. "Yes, Corporal," the major answered, not bothering to hide the weariness in his voice.

"Sir, from Lieutenant Liang," the man explained as he thrust a piece of paper towards the commanding officer.

Ping took the paper, then searched his pockets for his glasses. Not finding them, he called out, "Long?" He was about to call out again when he remembered that Private Long had been killed on the twentieth floor; she was hit by a spray of bullets from their own troops when two teams engaged the aliens from both ends of the same corridor. He shoved the paper back to the corporal, "What does it say?"

The non-com quickly unfolded the correspondence. "From Lieutenant Liang. Heavy losses on twenty-fifth floor. Enemy retreating; several wounded, one probable kill. Pursuing to twenty-six." He returned the paper to Ping.

Heavy losses, Ping thought. *How many more times can we say that?* He was still waiting on the report from the other stairwell, Lieutenant … what was his name? Jin? What news would Jin bring him?

He'd started out with nearly four hundred men, but now he was down to what? Fifty? Maybe another fifty walking-wounded; men who could barely carry their kit up another flight of stairs. Only five more floors until they reached the roof, but Ping doubted they would ever make it. Not at this rate.

And what about his opponents? His men had killed two and captured one, but how many more did they have? His lieutenants believed they had wounded some of the armored knights of the Commonwealth, but was it true? And even if that were true, had they disabled enough of them? His continuing losses seemed to argue they had not.

"Corporal, go down to the twentieth- floor. Find Sergeant Wu; tell him to bring up the prize," the major ordered. The man saluted and scampered off.

Ping considered his rapidly dwindling options. His surge up the tower was stalled, and the losses were crippling. *I need to do something*, he admitted to himself. *I just hope it's enough, because it is the only thing left.*

Commonwealth Office (level 25), Shanghai, PRC
2048APR21 10:44 CST (2048APR21 02:44 UTC)

Mackenzie kept up a steady rate of fire as she backpedaled up the corridor. "How are we doing, Lezhneva?"

The Base security guard had taken a round in the right arm; not fatal, but it was now impossible for her to lift her Type 3 with that hand. It also turned out that she was a lousy shot with her left, but she continued to snap off bolt after bolt, hoping to hit something as she hid behind Mackenzie for cover. "Doing fine, Chief," the woman lied, then corrected herself, "Sergeant."

"That's the spirit," Heather noted. "Harper?"

"Almost there," the private answered from her position in the converging corridor. She was facing an advancing force from the other stairwell. "Damn!" Harper exclaimed. "I'm out. Better hurry, I can't hold them anymore."

Time's up, the sergeant thought. "Run Lezhneva. I'll cover you." An icon on her helmet's faceplate display showed the unarmored crewman sprinting the final eight meters to the lift. Once she was halfway, Mackenzie picked up her own pace. Bullets pinged off her suit from two directions as she fell into the lift and the door closed. When she felt the car ascend, she let out a hearty sigh.

Regaining her feet, Mackenzie lifted the faceplate and turned on Harper, "Goddamn it, Private. How did you let your charge run out?"

"I've still got forty, Sarge. See for yourself," Harper answered, handing the sergeant her weapon. "The crystal fractured. Just like with Munoz."

Mackenzie inspected the weapon and found her private was correct; remaining charge in the power cells was 41% and the weapon's firing crystal had a 7 cm fracture at the aperture. If it weren't for the built-in safeties, the weapon could have exploded in Harper's hands.

"Take Lezhneva's gun; she's going up to see the doctor. Go with her," the sergeant ordered as the doors open on level twenty-six. "And make sure you get a fresh power pack."

"Yes, Sergeant. Come on, Mila," Harper replied as she aided the wounded Lezhneva.

Mackenzie stared at Harper's failed weapon and cursed. This was the fifth weapon taken out of action by a failed crystal. *If I make it out of this*, she thought, *those quality control people at Krieger Arms are going to get a letter from a very dissatisfied customer.* How could they design a weapon that can't survive a four-hour firefight? Shoddy workmanship, that's what it was. *And if I don't make it out of this, I'm going to haunt them!* She headed down the corridor to her next action.

Zhongshan Park, Shanghai, PRC
2048APR21 10:48 CST (2048APR21 02:48 UTC)

Chu Daxia could not believe the scene before her. When the helicopters fired on the building and shattered the reinforced windows, she had been surprised. But when a window suddenly blew out from one of the building's upper levels, she was shocked. *What is going on in there?* she wanted to scream. *And why did I have to insist on a morning run? Those are my people in there; I should be with them.*

When figures began to climb out of the shattered window and ascend the building, Chu grew concerned. At this distance, the lieutenant could not be certain if those were her troops in armor or some Chinese force attempting to capture the roof. Additional figures clarified the situation – while the first two figures awkwardly attempted to climb the ropes, the next two followed them up the ropes while firing their weapons at the leaders. At least until one of the stragglers was struck by a pulse gun bolt from the roof. Chu was ready to cheer until she saw the man plummet to the ground below. She could think of no worse way to die – fully aware of your fate and powerless to prevent it. When his partner met the same fate, she cast her eyes away. Chu had to remind herself that those were the enemy, that they would have not hesitated to see her Sentries meet the same exact fate. That was why they were out there.

She was relieved when the two Sentries finally reached the top and were dragged over the ledge to relative safety. Relative because she knew it was only a matter of time before the dead men's comrades fought their way to the roof.

Her eyes scanned the sky. Where were the fighters from before? Occasionally she caught a glint of sunlight reflecting oddly through the clouds. *Could that be them*? she wondered. If so, why didn't they get any closer? And how had the Chinese shot down one of the fighters? A thousand questions circled through her mind, and without comms she had no way of getting answers to any of them. All she could do was stand here in the park and watch helplessly.

Like Chu, Yang Xiwang also watched the activity on the damaged side of the black tower. With no word from the detachment's headquarters, she was left to speculate on what she was witnessing. The aliens were locked in battle with a local force using conventional weapons, and Yang had no doubt that those were Chinese soldiers, trained and armed by the

PLA. As yet another black-clad warrior fell from the building, the captain was certain that if she were to check the remains, she would find a weapon similar to her own. The body may be beyond recognition, but its equipment no doubt came from the same factory that supplied the PAP.

What are they thinking? she thought, though her face remained impassive. *They will bring down the wrath of the aliens on us all. How many more will die in response to this folly? And what madman approved this?*

Yang turned to look at the crowd behind their cordon. The crowd was larger now, no doubt the result of word spreading that something was happening at the tower. Something unusual. While most of the faces were elderly, there were more young faces than an hour ago. Still, the expression on those faces was simple curiosity. They were not rooting for any specific outcome, partly because they didn't understand what was happening but also because with communications down across the city, there was no chorus of voices telling them what outcome they should be cheering as patriots. There was no echo chamber of official outlets and their loyal followers pushing the people to rise up against foreign oppressors. Instead, they watched the spectacle as mere entertainment.

All except one face, she noted. The woman's eyes were partially shielded by the bill of her Shanghai Sharks cap, but it was still evident that those eyes were following the action around the tower far closer than any of her neighbors. There was also something about the way the woman held herself that did not say 'student' or 'office worker' to Yang. Indeed, the word that rose first in Yang's mind was 'soldier' – it was like watching one of her own people out of uniform.

The captain made eye contact with Sergeant Bo, and through subtle gestures made with her eyes and hands, drew Bo's attention to the young woman in question. Bo nodded, then grabbed two privates from the line, directing them to move into position. Careful not to alert her quarry, Yang eased closer until she was less than two meters away.

Chu finally noticed the movement of the officer, stealing a glance before averting her eyes to avoid drawing further scrutiny. Moving her head slowly, she finally noticed the other soldiers arrayed around her, ready to cut off any avenue of escape. She cursed herself for allowing herself to lose track of her surroundings; her concern for her platoon had pushed her own predicament from her mind. *Fool!*

The People's Armed Police captain stopped just out of reach, "Your identification, miss."

"*Wo bu mingbai*," Chu answered, hoping she might be able to hide her accent by passing for a Cantonese speaker from Hong Kong.

Yang smiled slightly, switching to English, "Fear no accent. Better than me English." She returned to the language they both knew best, "It will be easier if we speak naturally, despite your country dialect."

Chu nodded, then began to raise her hands.

Yang shook her head, gesturing for the lieutenant to return her hands to her sides. "That is not needed. I have no wish to alarm the aunties." She looked to the groups of older men and women watching their exchange from a distance. "You will come with me." Yang turned to lead Chu back towards the line of armed police restraining the crowd.

Chu Daxia noticed the three policemen moving closer, blocking any attempt at escape and guiding her to follow their superior. The lieutenant briefly considered using the crowd as a distraction, perhaps by knocking a few to the ground. But she dismissed this just as quickly; like the PAP captain, she had no desire to alarm the aunties, much less cause one real harm.

When they were finally away from the crowd, Yang turned to inspect their detainee. "What is your name?" she demanded.

Chu paused before deciding that equivocation would be futile. "Chu Daxia," she answered honestly. Of course, she was not obligated to provide more than the question required.

Yang looked to the tower hundreds of meters in the distance. "Are you a clerk? An office worker?"

The lieutenant shook her head, "I am a soldier. A Sentry."

"Good," Yang declared. "You do not lie to me. Why are you out here, and not with the others? Did you abandon your post?"

Chu grew angry, "I was out for a run. Exercise. When your people attacked, I was trapped outside."

Yang turned just as angry. "My people did not attack. We are here to protect you aliens. To make sure that you are not threatened by people who are tired of living under your control."

"Protect us from what? Where is the angry mob?" Chu demanded. She pointed to the crowd beyond the barricades, "Do you mean the aunties? Are they the threat?" She looked at Yang with contempt, "You certainly didn't protect us when your air force helicopters attacked."

The captain wanted to yell back that those helicopters were not Chinese, but she knew that was a lie. Who else had such aircraft in the area? It was the only possible answer, and they both knew it.

When Yang failed to respond, Chu spoke up. "Why don't you just lock me up with the pilot?"

That was precisely what she should do, Yang admitted. Turn the prisoner over to headquarters; make her their problem. But none of this felt right. "No," Yang answered slowly. "I want answers. And I think you can help me find them."

Commonwealth Office (level 28), Shanghai, PRC
2048APR21 10:54 CST (2048APR21 02:54 UTC)

Singh found the director standing in the corridor in a heated exchange with Doctor Zhao.

"Director, you're not listening," the diminutive woman declared. "We simply cannot keep moving the patients. Some of these wounds are barely set; carrying them upstairs is out of the question."

"Doctor, you're the one who is not listening," Quintilius asserted, the Roman woman towering over the doctor. "The enemy is only two levels below us. Leaving them here to be captured or killed is out of the question!"

Singh stepped up, hoping to solve this without further angering the woman he was assigned to protect. "Director, what's the problem?"

"Captain, finally," Argenta began. "Would you please explain to Doctor Zhao that we need to move her patients. The Chinese will be here in a less than an hour; maybe only thirty minutes." She crossed her arms. "I want the patients moved to our suite on twenty-nine."

Singh half-suspected that was the case. "Are you certain, ma'am?"

"Of course," Quintilius replied as if the question was absurd. "It is the most secure location in this building. Once it is locked, only the Regent or I can open it. It will be far less susceptible to their measures than the stairwell doors have proven."

Singh considered what he knew of the security measures around the Regent's chambers; it was probably harder to breach than the armories. He turned to Zhao, "She is correct, Doctor. We can't guarantee the safety of patients down here. It is in their best interest to move them."

Zhao remained just as adamant as the former executive director. "Moving them would risk additional injuries. In my opinion, the Chinese soldiers pose the lesser threat; I cannot believe they would harm injured combatants after they have laid down their arms."

Singh didn't have time for this. "Lieutenant, I didn't ask for your opinion," he announced, using Zhao's LTJG rank in place of her medical title. "We're moving them. That's an order."

Zhao's face turned red, "I do not report to you, Captain. As the senior medical officer for this facility, I am invoking my authority."

"Doctor, at the moment *I* am the senior officer in this building. Period!" Singh reminded the Han physician. "You can wait here for your Chinese cousins if you insist, but every one of those patients is being moved." He saw Zhao open her mouth to protest and cut her off. "If you don't like it, you can file a complaint with the director of security. I'll give you his contact info." Singh strode past Zhao and into one of the converted convalescent wards, "Listen up, people. We're moving everyone upstairs in three minutes. If you can walk, help the others who can't."

Zhao was furious, but held her tongue, instead walking to the other ward to repeat the captain's message.

Quintilius eyed the head of her security detail with a nod, "Captain, I believe you are spending too much time in the Regent's presence. You are picking up some bad habits." She reached out and patted his forearm, "Thank you."

Singh smiled politely, "Just remember, ma'am. You're going to be locked in there with the rest of them. For your safety and my peace of mind. No arguments."

"Of course," Argenta agreed, perhaps a little too willingly. "Once I know the patients are safe. You have my word."

Singh watched as Quintilius entered the ward to assist the patients, hoping that he had finally won an argument, but feeling it was just a bit too easy to be true.

CHAPTER 12

23rd Attack Squadron, 600 km south of Shanghai, PRC
2048APR21 02:59 UTC

SLDR Melina Dandoulaki was enjoying the quiet last minutes of high-altitude flight over the ocean when the familiar voice interrupted her.

"Black Hawk Leader, Black Hawk Two," her second-in-command announced. "Picking up three, repeat three, bogeys orbiting at angels-nine. Over."

Dandoulaki sighed slightly. Since viewing multiple entertainment videos featuring military aircraft from the planet below, FLT Rogers tended to lapse into the jargon of those fictional pilots. He even insisted that the rest of the squadron refer to him as *Steve* when his actual given name was Sylvester. *At least he didn't want to be called Buck*, Dandoulaki thought.

"Acknowledged, Black Hawk Two. Three U-A orbiting nine-zero-zero-zero," Melina translated for the benefit of the rest of the squadron. "Range?"

"Range five-two-seven, Black Hawk Leader," Rogers reported, returning to the approved script.

Dandoulaki appreciated the effort. "Black Hawk Leader to all Black Hawks. Maintain full shields below Mach 1." The only thing that allowed a bulky craft like their modified F-2 *Arrows* to fly at hypersonic speeds was the ability to alter their shield geometry to match the aerodynamic characteristics of a sewing needle. That, and the shield's ability to deflect any amount of heat from friction. And this ability was not a modification; all *Arrows* were capable of this. The modification to her squadron's aerospace craft was the enlarged ordnance bay that allowed them to carry more missiles than a standard F-2. That was key to their mission.

Minutes later, a ping in her helmet marked their arrival. "Black Hawks, descend to two-zero-zero-zero." Dandoulaki planned to blow past the unidentified aircraft (or *bogeys* as Rogers called them) at speed.

As they descended, Rogers reported from the lead fighter, "Black Hawks, I-D on bandits. Three J-three-one fighters; PLAAF I-F-F. Designated Panda One, Two and Three. They are painting."

The squadron leader noted the three icons on her display change color from yellow to red. At the same time, a warning that her own IFF was being interrogated. Melina hoped the Chinese pilots were smart enough to stay well away from the path of her squadron. At the Black Hawk's current speed, even advanced aircraft like the J-31 could get caught in their wake. As her altitude reached three thousand meters, Dandoulaki ordered, "Black Hawks Two through Five. Lock targets and confirm."

"Hawk Two; target locked," Rogers reported almost immediately.

"Hawk Three, locked," the next pilot answered, followed by Four and Five.

"Break formation at one-five-zero-zero. Hawk Six orbit for follow up," Dandoulaki instructed. If any of the five *Arrows* was unsuccessful in its attack, Black Hawk Six would be ready for a second try. Watching the altitude number reach the goal, she called out, "Break."

Swiping her hands along the controls, Melina shed speed while changing direction to allow her to sweep above the city below, adjusting her course to place her in line with her designated target. While others would focus on the telecom and bank buildings, she assigned the government building to herself. If anything did go wrong at the nearby hospital, she wanted the repercussions to come straight at her and not one of her pilots.

"Fox three," she heard Rogers call out. Then, "Missile away," from Black Hawk Four. Dandoulaki waited for the proper distance before releasing her missile. "Hawk One; fox three," she called out for Rogers' benefit, then banked right and climbed back up to two thousand meters, while her other two squadron mates reported their missile launches.

Noting one after another of the missiles detonate, Melina adjusted her comms channel and tested, "Black Hawk One to Castle Two, respond. Castle Two, this is Black Hawk One. Please respond." She waited ten seconds before repeating the hail, then another ten seconds before the third attempt. All with no answer from the Shanghai office. Dandoulaki checked her sensors; there was no sign of the comms interference they detected on their approach. *So why isn't the office responding?* she wondered. A sudden fear washed over her, *Are they all dead?*

That fear was allayed when a voice appeared, "Black Hawk One. Black Hawk One. This is Castle. Castle Two. Thank God!"

"Castle Two, good to hear your voice. You are instructed to contact Palace. Black Hawk will establish perimeter. Expect cavalry in twelve," the squadron leader instructed.

"Affirmative, Black Hawk. Nice to see a friendly face," the comms operator in the Commonwealth building replied.

"All Black Hawks. Panda flight is outbound. Repeat, outbound. No hostiles in range," the voice of Black Hawk Five announced.

Mission accomplished, Dandoulaki thought with a sigh of relief. At least the first part; now on to phase two. "Black Hawk One to Gold Eagle Three. Come on down; the coast is clear," she declared. Now all they had to do was maintain control of the airspace until the promised cavalry arrived.

Commonwealth Office (level 29), Shanghai, PRC
2048APR21 11:04 CST (2048APR21 03:04 UTC)

LTJG Hale nearly jumped when the sudden cheer rang out from the Sentry station on the top level. With the Chinese forces now battling the Sentries for control of level twenty-seven, the improvised operations room was abandoned. Now he had two comms operators crammed into a booth meant for one Sentry as they tried to direct the remaining Commonwealth forces defending the final two levels.

Wu Jing dashed out of the booth, looking around frantically. When she spotted Hale, she ran over and grabbed him by the arm, dragging him back to her lair, "Sir, the interference is gone. We can reach Terra Station again. They want to speak with you."

Rather than reprimand the young crewwoman for accosting an officer, Hale grabbed her in turn to hurry her along to the comms station, squeezing past her to enter the cramped space. "Where is it?" he demanded of the second technician.

Before the technician could answer, a voice on the speaker interrupted, "Have you found Commander Albrecht?"

Hale bent slightly towards the microphone on the panel, "I'm sorry; Commander Albrecht is not in the office right now. This is Lieutenant J-G Hale, operations officer," he informed the unfamiliar voice.

"Lieutenant, this is Admiral Derbez. What is your status?" the voice inquired.

"Sir!" Hale jumped to attention, having never dealt with any officer higher than a captain. "We are under attack by enemy forces, presumed to be Chinese PLA. They currently have control of level twenty-six through sub-level three; we control levels twenty-eight and higher. The annex remains secure to the best of my knowledge."

"Jesus!" a muffled voice exclaimed in the background. Derbez continued, "Hale, how many hostiles are you facing?"

"Unknown, sir," Hale replied. "They disable the sensors as they advance. We estimate the total number to be between three and five hundred." He realized how bad that sounded, "We've wounded a large number of those."

A new voice, a woman, jumped in, "Lieutenant Hale, this is General Graham. I need to speak with Lieutenant Chu."

Hales winced. "General, we don't know where Lieutenant Chu is; she was outside the building when the lock down occurred. Sergeant Mackenzie is in charge of the Sentries."

"Get him for me then," Graham ordered.

"Her, ma'am," Hale corrected. "Hold one." He nodded to the technician, who stabbed a few controls then nodded in return. "Sergeant, we have General Graham for you."

"Sergeant, sit rep," Graham barked without preamble.

"Station is almost lost, General. Minimum fifty hostiles. I have nine effectives. Five Sentry, one Base sec, one Comm sec, all in suits. Two base sec with sidearms only. Firefight on twenty-seven; will need to abandon soon to avoid capture."

"Casualties?" Graham demanded.

Mackenzie's voice returned, "Twenty-four wounded. Two dead. One Sentry, one Base sec. One Base supply clerk captured."

There was a sizeable delay before Graham responded. "Captain Bruttius and fourth platoon are inbound; ETA nine minutes," the general informed them. "Sergeant, you will hold until relieved."

"Understood, ma'am," Mackenzie answered without hesitation. "We hold."

The conversation returned to Admiral Derbez and Lieutenant Hale as Wu eased away from the doorway to the security booth. *Nine minutes*, she thought. Despite the confidence in SSGT Mackenzie's voice, a lot can happen in nine minutes.

Commonwealth Office (level 26), Shanghai, PRC
2048APR21 11:06 CST (2048APR21 03:06 UTC)

Major Ping Youxia was struggling with the railgun, trying to find a way to reach the trigger, but his gloves refused to fit within the trigger guard. In frustration, he pulled off the right glove and was finally able to work the trigger. Looking at his mismatched hands, he removed the other glove as well. Finally, the rifle felt comfortable in his hands. And more importantly, he could operate it.

Sergeant Wu arrived a few seconds later, placing the weapons power cell on the floor beside Ping with a noticeable thud. "This is the last," the weapons specialist informed the battalion commander. "Lieutenant Jin used the other one a few minutes ago upstairs."

A corporal came bounding out of the stairwell, nearly colliding with Wu as he skidded to a halt in front of the major. "Sir, listen," the man exclaimed, thrusting a radio into Ping's hand.

Ping held the device to his ear, frowning when he recognized voices issuing all too familiar orders while others responded to those commands. The communications jamming was gone, and Ping could now hear the People's Armed Police troops arrayed around the building take notice. Ping shook he head; he was out of time.

He handed the radio back to the corporal. "Find Lieutenant Jin; tell him to clear the route. And tell him to remind the men of their orders. All of their orders." The corporal nodded and ran off.

Ping picked up his helmet and placed it back on his head, finding it difficult to get it to sit correctly. He shrugged, there was nothing that could be done about it now. He lifted the railgun, cradling it in his arm and nodded to Wu to take the power cell. The cable between the two parts of the weapon gave them the appearance of mountaineers tethered to each other for safety. "Let's go."

Terra Station, Terra orbit
2048APR21 03:07 UTC

VADM Fitzpatrick was strategically positioned by the door of the operations center when the Regent came rushing up the corridor.

"Why didn't you tell me we got through?" he demanded. "I need to speak with her."

Fitzpatrick moved to the center of the corridor, her arms out at her sides to block the Regent's intended path. "No."

Rather than collide with the leader of his armed forces, the Regent was forced to come to an abrupt halt. "What?"

"No," the admiral repeated.

The Regent's eyes narrowed in rage, "Erin, get out of my way!"

"No!" Fitzpatrick shouted back. "Not until you calm down. Not until you start to care about *them* instead of just *her*," she declared. Pointing to the door to the operations center, "I can't let them see you like this. I can't let *her* see you like this!" The anger in her eyes far exceeded that of the Regent. "You're the goddamned leader of humanity! For once, could you make it look like the rest of us matter to you!"

"Admiral!" the Regent started, bellowing to outshout Fitzpatrick. Shaking his head, he turned and drove his right fist into the wall. Despite the material used in its construction, a considerable dent was left behind. Slowly, his rage faded, and his fists unclenched. "You're right," he croaked, his voice cracking. "Oh God! I have to stop doing this." He finally turned to face her, "I'm sorry."

Fitzpatrick exhaled and relaxed her own fists, happy to see that she would not have to commit career suicide. "Good. Then I won't have to give you a thumping," she said with relief.

The Regent looked at her askance, "You and what navy, Admiral?"

Fitzpatrick smiled gently now that the man was returning to his normal inappropriate ways. "Don't worry. I had them turn off the security cameras in the corridor. I didn't want to embarrass you."

"You mean there would be no evidence for your court martial," the Regent tossed back.

Fitzpatrick shook her head, "Well, if you can behave yourself, you can go in now."

The Regent shrugged, "No rush."

"You know you can't fool me," the admiral admonished him as she walked to the operation center door. "How's the hand? That looked like it hurt."

The Regent flexed his right hand, hoping he successfully hid the wince. "It's fine," he lied and followed her. He made sure to keep his eagerness in check. *I'll be OK*, he thought, *and now Argenta will as well.*

Commonwealth Office (level 28), Shanghai, PRC
2048APR21 11:11 CST (2048APR21 03:11 UTC)

"Ma'am, it's time to go," CAPT Singh shouted from the corridor. The sound of weapons fire in the stairwell nearly drowning him out as he kept a wary eye on both directions.

"They need this equipment," Quintilius shouted back. "I will not have someone die now when rescue is so close." She pointed to the small pile of medical equipment she had created on the floor. "Now, are you going to help me, or do I carry it all myself?"

Cursing under his breath, Singh rushed in and grabbed two of what he hoped were the heavier items, "Fine. Let's go!"

They stepped into the corridor to the sound of heavy footfalls approaching them. Singh shoved the director behind him as he took a shooting stance with his sidearm. Much to his relief, the figure that emerged was wearing Sentry armor.

"What's wrong with you people?" Mackenzie's voice blasted from her suit's external speakers. "We lost the north stairs. Move it!"

Singh holstered his weapon and retrieved the infirmary equipment he'd dropped a second earlier when he heard a familiar ping. All heads turned towards the lifts fifteen meters down the hall.

"Now what?" Mackenzie cursed, then froze in place as an unfamiliar figure exited the lift car. At first, seeing the familiar green armor, she thought it was one of her team. Though none of her people should have been behind her. But the figure wasn't entirely familiar – the boots and helmet were black, and the weapon was unfamiliar. But it was the face that was most out of place. Without a faceplate attached to the helmet, she had no trouble realizing that this was not one of her men.

The sergeant snapped her gun up at the same time the stranger raised his weapon. Squeezing the trigger, Heather was rewarded not with a blinding flash of energy, but with a dozen flashing red indicators on her helmet display. Just as with Harper, her Type 3 pulse gun chose the absolute worst time to fail her. With a shout of disgust, she broke into a run, planning to drive the shattered crystal of her rifle through the stranger's face.

Before she covered five meters, the air around her exploded and she felt a searing pain in her chest and found herself lying flat on her back, staring at the ceiling. Looking down her chest, she spotted the metal bolt protruding from her armored chest plate, just slightly to the right and still glowing red hot. *Or is the red my blood?* she wondered as she noticed liquid oozing down the side.

Singh dropped his bundles and drew his weapon, pulling the director down behind him. She was too stunned to speak as he fired shot after shot against the green intruder who tossed away his strange rifle. Singh's bolts struck their mark but proved useless until he struck a second figure as he emerged from behind the first, this one dressed in black as all other intruders had been. Singh cursed his training when he realized he was targeting the center of mass as he'd always been taught. Before the security captain could attempt a head shot at the now grinning face, his opponent replied with a hail of bullets from the automatic carbine that his now deceased partner provided.

Singh fell back in a heap, his legs suddenly on fire. His right hand searched the ground frantically as he tried to recover the sidearm that skittered away when he hit the floor. When he heard heavy footsteps near, he twisted his head to catch sight of Quintilius. Even after all this, what caused his heart to sink was the sight of blood staining her suit from more than one wound. His head snapped forward again as a heavy boot crushed his right hand.

"You can live," the man standing above him declared in heavily accented English, then stepped past Singh to reach the director.

"Leave her alone," Singh yelled at the top of his lungs, now aware of blood in his mouth.

"Quiet, alien," Major Ping ordered as he pressed his weight back onto Singh's hand. Returning his attention to Quintilius, Ping raised his rifle, "You are Regent's bitch. He hides. You die."

Singh was ready to yell again when a blur of green flew over him.

With her right hand, Mackenzie reached over the armored man's shoulder and pulled the carbine's short muzzle up just as a stream of bullets stitched the ceiling. With her left hand, she drove Singh's missing pistol under Ping's helmet, pressing the discharge crystal to the base of his neck. With a scream, she held down the trigger and fell backwards. Instantly, the weapon's beam sliced through flesh as Heather swept the gun across the width of the helmet.

When the two armored bodies fell, they landed in a pile on Singh's ruined legs. Again, the security captain shrieked, while the Chinese major's severed head bounced once before rolling down the corridor.

Somehow fittingly, as the sound of Singh's latest scream passed, the echoes of weapons fire from the stairwell also began to fade.

CHAPTER 13

11th Transport Squadron, 800 m above Shanghai, PRC
2048APR21 03:12 UTC

As he did on most flights, SGT Pandey was resting his eyes when the voice of the pilot interrupted his silent contemplation. "Sergeant, we're on approach. I'm tying you into the coms channel."

"Understood," he replied, his eyes never opening or even flicking from side to side. This was all part of the pattern he had developed over the years. Rest when you are able, because soon there will be no rest. After a click, a second voice entered his helmet.

"Gold Bear Four. Confirm roof is secure; landing pad is clear for your use," the newcomer announced.

The pilot's voice replied, "Understood, Castle. We will use pad as jump zone." Because their launch was larger and heavier than the standard shuttlecraft, the launch could not land on the roof. Instead, it would hover a meter or two over the landing pad and the Sentries would jump down individually, protected by their armored suits.

"Gold Bear Four. Be advised, wind speed is increasing. Hover is not advised at this time," the voice of the Shanghai office returned, and Pandey was now able to identify her as CRW1 Wu.

"Castle, this is Sergeant Pandey. Is hover cleared above five meters?" he asked, assuming that the concern was that a sudden gust could crash the launch into the building before the pilot could compensate.

There was a moment before Wu returned, "Gold Bear Four. Hover above six meters is advised."

Now it was the pilot who paused. "Sergeant, how much will your team drift in a 6-meter fall?"

With practiced eye movements combined with subtle motions of his gloved hands, Pandey brought up his suit's tactical computer to make the calculations. He understood the pilot's concern – just as the wind could throw the launch into the building, it could also change the course of his Sentries as they fell to the roof. A little wind and they'd be scatter across the roof; too much and they could miss entirely. Their suits were rated for heights up to nine meters in a 1 G fall. Add another ninety or so meters to that, and the survival rate dropped rapidly. "One to two meters, depending on the direction of the wind," Pandey answered, adding, "at currently reported windspeed."

In the cockpit, the pilot considered the risks. "Understood. We'll try to give you a cushion. Castle, will hover at six meters. Clear your people as much as possible. Now at one-four-zero."

"Confirmed, Gold Bear Four. You are clear to hover," Wu answered.

Seconds later, the red light next to the left-side hatch lit up and the nine Sentries in the passenger compartment stood. As their leader, Pandey had the option of being the first out of the door, or the last. Given the circumstances, he opted to go last since the likelihood of a sudden gust increased as the launch tried to maintain its position. He'd rather go over the side himself than watch helplessly as one or more of his troops fell to their death.

"Thompson, your team first. Then Mourad's," the sergeant instructed as the door opened and they could feel the force of the wind. When the light changed from red to green, he yelled, "Go!"

Each of the green-suited Sentries clutched his or her rifle and hopped out of the open hatchway at five second intervals. With the last one clear, Pandey followed his troops' example and jumped.

Commonwealth Office (level 30/roof), Shanghai, PRC
2048APR21 11:14 CST (2048APR21 03:14 UTC)

Pandey landed with a thud; when he tried to take a step back to steady himself, he kicked a short wall that turned out to be the edge of the roof. Steeling himself, he looked over the edge at the fate he avoided seconds earlier. *It is a blessing that heights do not frighten me*, he thought.

A fellow Sentry in battle-scarred armor rushed up to him, "Sergeant Pandey."

With their faceplates polarized, Pandey could not identify the man. While the single diagonal stripe on his sleeve marked him as a corporal, his nameplate was the victim of multiple strikes from Chinese bullets. "Corporal …," Pandey attempted.

"Creticus. Corporal Creticus," the man answered, leading Pandey towards the building's rooftop entrance where his teams were assembled. Creticus looked up, scanning the sky, "Where's the rest of the platoon? Where's the captain?"

Pandey stopped at the entrance, answering, "Don't worry. They're on their way. We're just the first wave." He paused, "Where is Sergeant Mackenzie?"

"I don't know," Creticus replied. "The last report had her on level twenty-eight, before the Chinese cut the sensors."

Pandey waved to his corporals, "Thompson, take your team to the north stairwell; Mourad, you have the south. We're retaking the building. Go!" He watched as the two groups trotted off in different directions to begin their assault. Returning his attention to Creticus, "Take me to our command post. I'm taking charge until we find Mackenzie."

"Yes, Sergeant," the Roman corporal answered, and the two men bounded down the stairs to the level below.

Zhongshan Park, Shanghai, PRC
2048APR21 11:18 CST (2048APR21 03:18 UTC)

"Captain Yang, I need information. We are detecting additional spacecraft in your area," the voice on her radio announced. "Can you identify the type? What are they doing?"

Yang regretted the sudden restoration of communications near the black tower. Ever since Sergeant Bo informed her of this change, she had multiple superior officer's contacting her. The latest, Major Ding, was stationed in the detachment's headquarters building and apparently assigned to monitor aircraft. "Major," she replied, "I am not an expert in spacecraft types, nor was I able to view any details from my position. What I could see was an object appear above the tower. It then landed on the roof and departed a minute later." Yang truly hoped that would satisfy the major so she could get back to her real work.

"Did they unload anything? Soldiers or equipment? Was it carrying people away?" Ding pressed her.

Yang shook her head, glad that Ding could not see her frustration, "Major, the building is one hundred meters tall, and I am on the ground in its shadow. I could not tell you if the vehicle even had doors. I am sorry."

"Very well, Captain. I will check with other units in the area," Ding conceded. "But if you do learn anything, contact me immediately. And keep your eyes open; we are tracking a second vehicle approaching your position." The man closed the connection without another word.

Relieved, the captain reattached the radio to her vest, then walked over to her Commonwealth … detainee; she really couldn't call the woman her prisoner. "What was that thing on the roof?"

Chu Daxia continued to look up at the building as she answered, "Too large to be a shuttlecraft. It might have been a launch, maybe a lighter." She looked at Yang and shrugged, "Hard to tell when all you can see is the landing gear."

Yang studied the woman, "Even harder to tell when you are ordered to conceal strategic information."

Chu refused to rise to the bait, remaining silent as she turned her eyes back to the Commonwealth tower.

Yang thought of pressing the issue when she noticed a shadow passing overhead. Looking up, she spotted an odd sight – an airplane without wings. At least that was her first impression; whatever it was, it looked for all the world like a modern airliner fuselage, but in place of the normal massive wings, this object sported stubby fins towards what she assumed was the rear. And it was moving very slowly in the air, silently hovering like a blimp. As it grew larger, she realized it was planning to land in the field she now occupied.

"Attention. Attention. Clear the immediate area," a voice from above boomed in Chinese, then repeated the instruction in English.

Yang barely registered this as Chu grabbed her arm and yelled, "Move!" The two women dashed away from the pseudo-dirigible as it grew nearer, incidentally running towards the black tower. Sergeant Bo and the private he'd brought along as an escort broke into a run to keep up with them.

After twenty meters, they all stopped and turned around to check on their pursuer. Even before the spindly landing gear of the bulky craft touched down in the grass, large doors on both sides opened and green-colored stormtroopers popped out. With the tinted facemasks on their green helmets, Yang could not see the faces of the people in those suits, but she already knew who they were – this was the Commonwealth's army. The aliens were invading her city in force.

As the soldiers landed, they formed a line on either side of their vehicle, facing the tower. The PAP private with the small group moved to raise his rifle, but Bo wisely clamped a hand on the man's arm and forced the weapon down. As if in response, one of the green-suited soldiers broke rank and walked slowly up to them, its weapon at the ready.

Captain Yang stepped forward and the soldier stopped two meters away. The soldier's helmet suddenly switched from tinted to transparent, revealing a woman, likely of Indian descent. "You'll have to withdraw. We are securing this area."

"I am Captain Yang of the People's Armed Police. This park is already secured under our authority. You have no business landing that," she gestured to their vehicle, "… thing here."

The woman in the green armor smiled politely, "Captain, I am Corporal Sharma, Solar Guard First Ranger Battalion. Everything within one kilometer of the Commonwealth office has been declared a Commonwealth exclusion zone. That includes this park." She turned to scan the array of PAP troops in the distance. "This has been communicated to your government in Beijing; I suggest you contact them for confirmation. But you and your people will do that over there," she pointed towards Yang's troops some distance away.

Yang stood her ground … literally, "Corporal, I want to speak with your commanding officer."

Chu stepped forward, "Corporal, I am Lieutenant Chu Daxia, Third Sentry; assigned to SCO Shanghai."

Sharma eyed the other woman skeptically, then toggled a control on her in-helmet display, "Captain? I have a woman here claiming to be a Lieutenant Chu from your unit." Her eyes wavered as she listened to the response the others could not hear. "Understood," she answered, then returned her focus to Yang and Chu. "Wait here," she said as she held up her hand and backed away to stand another two meters closer to her lander.

After a moment, a new, taller green knight marched up to the group, like Sharma stopping two meters away. "Chu?" the man asked as he cleared his faceplate's shading.

Sheepishly, Chu removed the Sharks cap from her head. After all this time, she had forgotten it was there to shield her appearance. "Yes, sir."

"Why are you out here? Dressed like that?" the captain demanded. "This isn't your day off, Lieutenant."

"Yes, sir. Sorry, sir," Chu replied like a cadet being reprimanded, snapping to attention despite her attire. "I was out for a run when the office was locked down."

"Unbelievable," the senior officer muttered before turning his attention to the uniformed woman. "And you are?"

Chu jumped in, "Captain Bruttius, may I introduce Captain Yang of the People's Armed Police." She explained to Yang, "Captain Bruttius is in command of the Sentries assigned to the office."

"Captain," Bruttius acknowledged his counterpart warily in Chinese. "I understand you are questioning our presence. While I am not looking for a confrontation with the local police, I am also not going to allow any delays in my actions. Please return to your troops and keep them out of my way."

"Captain Bruttius," Yang started with a little difficulty pronouncing the Roman's name, "I am not here to interfere, but I cannot ignore my orders. I am to determine just what is happening in *our* city." She looked back at Bo and the private, "My men will return to our positions, but I must accompany you in order to report back to my superiors."

Bruttius shook his head, "I'm not allowing armed police to enter a Commonwealth facility."

Yang paused for only a second, then reached across her body with her left hand and withdrew her pistol from its holster. Handing the weapon to Bo, she turned back towards Bruttius, "Now what is your objection?"

Bruttius grimaced, then folded. "Very well, you can act as an observer. But you follow any instruction given to you by me or any other Guardian. Understood?" He turned his attention to Chu, then called back to Sharma, "Corporal, get the lieutenant a sidearm."

Another soldier rushed up, announcing, "Captain, we're ready to move in."

Bruttius nodded. "Lieutenant Baquero, meet my deputy, Lieutenant Chu," he declared, gesturing to the woman in the running shorts. "Make sure she doesn't get her head blown off before her hearing." He pointed to the two Chinese women, "And you two, at the first sign of shooting, you get behind the Sentries and Rangers. Unlike us, you two are not bullet-proof." With that, he stepped past the two women. "Move out!"

Chu hurried to keep up with her commander, as Baquero moved closer. "I'm sure your CO was just joking about the hearing," the second lieutenant offered. She extended a gloved hand, "Inez Baquero; First Rangers."

Chu accepted the handshake, answering, "Chu Daxia; Third Sentries." In a lower tone, she added, "For now."

Commonwealth Office (level 28), Shanghai, PRC
2048APR21 11:21 CST (2048APR21 03:21 UTC)

It took Pandey's fresh troops five minutes of fierce fighting to help push the Chinese forces back down the south stairwell; another two minutes to clear the north stairwell down to twenty-seven. CPL Thompson moved down the corridor on twenty-eight cautiously, ready for any enemy stragglers lying in wait. When she turned the corner, the sight before her brought her up short. She rushed to the woman lying in a pool of blood, pulling her glove off to check for a pulse.

A few meters away, a man lay outstretched under two armored bodies. As she moved closer, she noticed that the body at the top of the pile was missing its head. She nearly jumped when a hand grabbed her leg.

"Help," Singh implored with a croaking voice. "Doctor."

Thompson stared down at the man, finally recognizing the head of the Regent's protective detail. She toggled her comms, "Sergeant! I need a doctor on twenty-eight. Fast! Two civilians, and two of our own." She peered back at the headless body, trying to make out the nameplate. "And Sergeant, Ngaporo is dead."

Pandey squeezed past a Base security guard to reach the scene. "How is she?"

Dr. Zhao continued to work on the woman while answering, "Captain Singh is stabilized, though I'm not sure we can save the leg. As for the director," she paused and looked up. "I've done what I can, but there's a lot of internal damage. And we exhausted my supplies a while ago."

Pandey silently cursed himself for not thinking to bring medical supplies with them. Of course, none of his superiors thought of it either, but that was hardly comforting. He thought of the C-9 *Owl*, now parked in the field below. Only ninety or so meters away, but it might as well be ninety kilometers. There was no way to reach it in time, and it was far too big to land on the roof. There was only one choice. Switching channels, he ordered, "Wu, contact Gold Bear Four. We need immediate medivac to the nearest surgical facility. Priority Omega!"

"Sir?" the young Base comms technician replied.

"Just do it!" Pandey barked, not willing to discuss this now. He bent down to address Zhao, "Do what you can. I'll need you to go with them once the launch is here. It'll probably be Terra Monitor East Asia; Australia would take longer."

"Sergeant, I can't go. I have too many patients here as it is," Zhao complained. "Unless you plan to evacuate all of the wounded."

Pandey was getting tired of Base personnel who didn't seem to understand the situation. "Doctor, right now you have one patient. The director. The other patients can be seen by your corpsmen; you need to do whatever you can to keep *her* alive. She is your top priority. Is that clear?"

Zhao stood up, "Sergeant, maybe you haven't noticed, but these stripes aren't decorations. I outrank you."

Pandey shook his head. "Until Captain Bruttius arrives, or we find Lieutenant Chu, I am the senior Guardian on site. And we are in charge during an attack, no matter the rank." He moved to continue down the corridor, "And a piece of advice, Lieutenant. Never argue with the person who has all the guns."

"Sergeant Mackenzie is over here," Thompson stated flatly, hoping to not further fan Pandey's wrath. She gestured to the armored form with the metal rod protruding from her chest, rather than the one missing its head.

With her helmet removed, Pandey was able to stare down into the frozen face of his friend. *At least she went out fighting*, he thought as his eyes drifted to the numerous marks and dents in her armor, finally settling on the single long bolt now fused with her chest plate. *She would have preferred that to dying in her sleep.* He offered a silent prayer for his friend's next life, smiling briefly when he remembered how angry that concept would make her.

"So, this must be Ngaporo," the sergeant declared as he moved to the other body in Guard armor.

Thompson shook her head, "That's what it says on his armor, but it's not Ngaporo."

Pandey studied the second corpse, noting the armor was just as scarred as Mackenzie's. Looking back to Thompson in confusion, "How can you tell?"

The corporal led him a few meters down the corridor where an odd black helmet lay, resting against the wall. With her foot, she nudged the object until it rotated to reveal that the helmet was not empty.

Pandey stared down into the lifeless eyes as they looked back from the ashen face. "You're right; that's not Ngaporo," he agreed dryly. He looked up, then canvassed the corridor for any other clues. "So now the question is – who in the twenty-one hells of Naraka is it?"

CHAPTER 14

Commonwealth Office (level 0/ground), Shanghai, PRC
2048APR24 11:24 CST (2048APR21 03:24 UTC)

Bruttius removed his right glove and placed his palm against the door plate, announcing "Release all locks, level zero. Authorization: Bruttius one-seven-gamma-four-two-nine-theta."

He was rewarded with an audible clunk and the synthetic voice of the office's computer in response, "Access granted. Transferring control to Bruttius, Attalus; Captain, Third Sentry Battalion."

"Go," he ordered Baquero, who rushed through the now open doorway, her teams spreading about the lobby. The captain held Chun and Yang back until a green telltale informed him that the ground level of the Commonwealth building was secure. "OK. Remember, stay with the Rangers." he ordered as he led the small group into the building.

Even though she knew she shouldn't be, Chu was amazed by the damaged walls and ceilings of the lobby she passed through only this morning. Most of the damage was lines of bullet holes from the automatic weapons fire, though there were more than a few scorch marks from the pulse guns employed by her Sentries and others. Completing the scene of carnage was around two dozen bodies, most lying in circles of dried blood on the pseudo-marble flooring. Unlike the battle damage, all the bodies wore black fabric uniforms and matching helmets; none were in the familiar green hard shell her Sentries wore in combat. She was relieved at least, at that.

"Captain," Baquero called out, "You should see this."

Bruttius led his group to the wall where the lieutenant was standing. There on the floor was yet another body, propped up as it leaned against its final resting place. The thing that set this body apart was its pristine condition. No dried blood surrounded it; indeed, there were no visible wounds anywhere, just eyes frozen in terror and remnants of spittle on the front of the dead man's combat vest.

Bruttius looked to Yang. "One of yours?"

Yang pondered the sight. "May I?" she asked the Commonwealth captain, gesturing to the body. Bruttius nodded. She bent lower, tilting her head from side to side as she examined the man before her. Slowly, she grasped the man's weapon by the barrel, being careful not to do anything that would cause the muzzle to focus on the living soldiers in the lobby. She unhooked the gun from the dead man's harness, then removed the magazine and ejected any remaining rounds from the chamber with practiced ease.

Standing, Yang examined the weapon more closely. "Standard QBZ-44B carbine; nothing unusual. It is used by our forces as well as several neighboring nations." she announced, then paused in puzzlement, "Odd. The production number is missing." She held the now inert weapon out to the Roman, indicating where the identifier should be.

Bruttius accepted the rifle and looked for himself. "Removed somehow?" he asked.

Yang shook her head, "More like it was never there. But that should be impossible." She inspected one of the cartridges she ejected earlier. "DBP41 round; used by special operations forces," she declared handing this to Bruttius as well. "Again, nothing unusual. Except for the missing number."

Bruttius accepted her explanation without comment, gesturing to the body, "And him?"

Here Yang was less certain, "He is Han Chinese. The uniform looks very much like the style worn by the Sea Dragon team. But there are no markings – no unit badge, no rank, no name. I cannot say who this is. He could be PLA ground force or PLAN Marine; he could be a mercenary."

The Roman was less happy with this description. "And what killed him?" he asked, pointing to the pristine uniform. "It certainly wasn't weapons fire."

"Poison," Yang declared without pause. "And recently. There is an odor if you get close enough; perhaps your doctors can identify the precise agent used."

Bruttius stared at her, "Are you suggesting that he committed suicide rather than allow himself to be captured?"

Now Yang was confused, "Of course. It is a common practice among fanatics throughout the region." She looked at him quizzically, "How are you not familiar with this?"

Bruttius shrugged, "To be honest, I did not think you Earth Terrans had that level of commitment." He turned to review the number of bodies scattered around the lobby. "It makes you sound almost Roman."

Terra Monitor East Asia, Terra orbit
2048APR21 04:07 UTC

The Regent paced nervously as shuttlecraft *Erin* rose into the hangar bay. "Come on, come on," he mumbled as he waited for the hatch to open, drawing even more impatient when the gentle rocking indicated that the auxiliary craft was settled on the deck.

Following the leads of Director Jiang and VADM Fitzpatrick, SGT Amani said nothing to the leader of the Commonwealth during the 46-minute journey from Terra Station. With the signal from the cockpit, Amani pressed a control and announced, "Arrived."

The Regent leapt from the shuttlecraft, crossing the hangar deck and through the airlock into the station's labyrinth of corridors. Jiang and Fitzpatrick rose slowly from their seats and exchanged a knowing look, then followed their leader at a more relaxed pace. They knew exactly where the man was going, so there was no need to attempt to overtake him.

"Thank you, Sergeant," Fitzpatrick said as she reached the hatch. "And again, mention this to no one."

"Mention what, ma'am?" Amani asked with convincing surprise.

The Regent was pacing in the infirmary's waiting area when the director and admiral rejoined him. The only thing that was forcing him to wait there was the fact that the operating room doors stubbornly refused to open for him, and the staff stubbornly refused to address this issue despite his numerous and sometimes ominous threats if they did not rectify the situation.

"Regent," Jiang beckoned him as she entered the area. "A word, please."

The Regent spun around, closing the gap between himself and the head of Commonwealth defense, "I don't want to hear it, Director. Don't remind me of my responsibilities."

"Not at all, Regent," Jiang began calmly. "I merely wish to remind you that this area, like many secure sections of the station, is under constant video surveillance for reasons of security. If you persist in your actions, I will see to it that Director Quintilius receives a complete, unedited copy of this material at her earliest opportunity." She stared up into the Regents eyes with cold intent. "Now. Sit. Down!"

The Regent fumed silently for a minute, calculating how he would punish Jiang for this later, then threw his body into the nearest chair.

Fitzpatrick crossed the waiting room's threshold from the corridor where she had been standing and paused besides Jiang. "Impressive," she declared softly, then moved to take the chair next to the Regent. "Feeling better, sir?" she inquired.

The Regent turned his head only slightly, and answered through gritted teeth, "Not now, Erin. Not if you know what's good for you." His hand was in constant motion, nervously tapping on the arm of his chair.

Fitzpatrick maintain a genial air. "Well, there's the problem. My da always said I just didn't know when to quit." She looked around the room. "So, I'm just going to have to keep this up until you see reason."

The Regent shook his head. "Where's the damned doctor?" he grumbled.

"With the damned patient. Obviously. Exactly where he's supposed to be," the admiral answered, ignoring the idea that the question could be rhetorical. "What did you think? They're just going to drop everything because the bloody emperor is in the lobby?"

"You do know that I can still fire you?" the Regent threw back, his frustration quickly transferring from the medical staff to the admiral.

Fitzpatrick laughed, "You threaten that every year. And you never go through with it." She crossed her arms and leaned back, "It loses its punch when I know you're bluffing."

The Regent's hand stopped tapping. "Why do I put up with you?" he demanded in an overloud voice.

"Because I'm your friend," Fitzpatrick fired back at equal volume. "And let's face it, it's not a job most people are fighting for. Just between you and me, you're a bit of an arse!"

The Regent stood, rounding on Fitzpatrick in fury … and burst out laughing. He laughed for over a minute, at one point leaning over to support himself by the arm of his chair while trying to catch his breath. When he finally regained control, he stood up and stared at the ceiling. "God, you're right. I'm a son of a bitch."

Fitzpatrick stood as well, "Well, I make it a point never to argue with you when you're right. Luckily, it doesn't happen that often."

The Regent looked at his friend of over thirty years and extended his hand, "Thank you."

Erin took the offered hand, grasping the Regent's wrist in the Roman fashion. "Just doing my job, sir. Protecting the Commonwealth from the mad king."

"Yessss," the Regent agreed, drawing the word out. "I really do have to stop doing that."

"I know I would appreciate that," Jiang commented a few meters away.

The Regent turned to the voice, "Thank you, also, Jiang Weijia. I know I don't make your life easy."

"No, sir," she confirmed.

He spread his arms wide, "Hug?"

Jiang's eyes narrowed. "No, sir," she repeated.

Any further discussion of the Regent's numerous failings was postponed when a small Japanese woman dressed in pale green surgical gear stepped out of the operating room. "Regent?" she beckoned.

He crossed the room quickly with his entourage in tow. "How is she? Are you the surgeon?"

The woman nodded, "Doctor Arimura, sir. The director is stable for now. Please understand, there was extensive damage and a significant amount of blood loss. I was able to repair much of the damage … but she will require additional procedures."

"But she'll live. She's going to be OK," the Regent pressed.

Arimura remained reserved, "I believe she will survive; we'll know better in a few hours. You should know, there was some damage to the spine. Given her age, it's possible she may not recover completely, particularly in the area of mobility."

"Are you saying she can't walk?" he begged, fear creeping into his voice.

"We just don't know yet. She's resting right now. When she wakes, we will be able to run additional tests. Even if there is some initial impairment, it's not uncommon to see improvement over time," Arimura answered.

The Regent took a step back, "What you're telling me is: you don't know."

Arimura tried to be more reassuring. "We don't know *yet*, sir. I'm sorry, I wish I could tell you everything is going to be fine. But these things take time."

"If it would help, I can arrange for our usual doctor … Doctor Nonius," he paused as if rethinking his words. "I can have her brought here to assist you …"

"I have already consulted with Doctor Nonius to review the director's medical history," Arimura informed the Regent, with no hint that she was offended by the suggestion. "You are welcome to bring her here to review the case and assist in the recovery process. But I assure you, Regent, we are providing the best care possible."

The Regent nodded, taking a deep breath and seeking calm. "Alright, Doctor. I understand." He hoped that sounded more convincing to the women around him than it did in his head. "Can I see here?"

"As I said, she is resting now. And we have the director in a sterile environment to prevent infection," the doctor explained. "The most we can offer right now is a video feed. Should I arrange that?"

The Regent shook his head, "No. No, I'll wait until she is awake."

"Of course, sir," the doctor agreed. "We will contact you at Terra Station in a few hours."

"Not necessary, Doctor. I'll be here on the station. At least until Argenta is able to travel," he announced. He shook the doctor's hand and moved towards the exit.

Jiang and Fitzpatrick hurried to keep up. "Sir?" Jiang inquired.

"I can do my job anywhere, Director," he answered. "One space station is much like the rest. All I need is an office with a communications setup. So, let's go find one."

Terra Monitor East Asia, Terra orbit
2048APR21 05:30 UTC

Unlike the large, modular space stations orbiting Earth, Mars and Jupiter, Terra Monitor East Asia was a single-module compact station designed for one purpose – to protect the planet below. As such, its facilities for visitors ran the gamut from very limited to non-existent. There were no guest quarters since no one had considered the idea of someone visiting the monitor for any length of time. CDR Jefferson was able to arrange two junior officer quarters, currently unoccupied while replacement personnel were in transit from the admiral's planet of Sserllich-Haash Four.

It was decided that Jiang and Fitzpatrick would alternate days, one assisting the Regent on the monitor station, while the other returned to Terra Station to resume her normal schedule (if anyone's schedule can be considered normal near the zenith of an interplanetary government). So it was the admiral who was shown the designated quarters. After a quick inspection of that broom closet, Erin fondly recalled her quarters on *Enterprise* when she commanded that ship. *At least there I could turn around without opening the door*, she grimaced. *Oh well, lowly ensigns don't get those perks, and now, neither do I.*

The Regent ignored his temporary quarters, choosing instead to camp out in a nearby conference room that had also been appropriated for his use. A Sentry stood guard at the door to prevent anyone from mistakenly interrupting the leader of the Commonwealth. Recognizing the admiral as she approached, the woman activated the door and nodded, watching Fitzpatrick pass through before resealing the door and resuming her post.

The Regent failed to look up as he sat at the table in the center of the room, intently studying the contents of a tablet he gripped in both hands. Fitzpatrick looked to her right to find one of the Regent's assistants seated at a side table. "Miss Nnaji, how was the flight?"

The young Nigerian woman smile brightly, "Very nice, Admiral, thank you. Just a bit rushed." Nnaji had been flown up on short notice from the New York office to join the Regent in his new command center, as it were.

"Have they found you quarters yet?" Erin inquired.

"Not yet," the woman answered. "One of the chief petty officers offered to vacate her quarters, but the executive officer is still trying for something a little closer to the office." She gestured to include their current location.

"If you two are done commenting on our accommodations, some of us are trying to run the Commonwealth," the Regent declared.

With a raised eyebrow to Nnaji, Fitzpatrick turned to approach the table, placing a tablet on the surface and taking a seat across from the Regent. "I didn't want to disturb the great man."

"Oh, Erin," he returned, still focused on his tablet, "You know I've always found you disturbing." With a flourish, he deactivated the device and placed it face down on the table. "Coffee?"

"Always," Fitzpatrick answered as the Regent rose and walked to a table in the corner opposite his assistant. Lifting a carafe, he poured the contents into a mug, frowning when the vessel ran dry. He turned to Nnaji, waving the now empty coffee carafe in the air, "Another pot, Chika. In fact, better make it two."

"Already on its way," Nnaji answered, never looking up from her computer.

The Regent returned to the table, delivering the half-full mug of coffee to Fitzpatrick. "And that's why I need her here. She knows what I need before I need it." His face froze, then the smile slipped. "Any word on Ji-Hyun?" he asked softly. His other assistant had been in the Shanghai office at the time of the attack.

Fitzpatrick nodded, "Miss Son is fine. A little shaken, but that is to be expected. I've arranged for her to have two weeks leave to spend with her family in Korea." She nudged the tablet she'd brought across the table.

The Regent lifted the offered device, smiling gently, "Good. She deserves it. All the people there deserve it. They should all get four weeks leave. Eight! Hell, I deserve two weeks leave, and I wasn't even there."

He stopped when he realized he was rambling. "Ahh, I can't even get two hours leave."

"Yes, sir. You are the true victim in all of this," the admiral mocked him.

The Regent activated the device and perused the contents, "This can't be right." He flicked through several pages, "I don't understand. How?" He turned the device to show the information to Fitzpatrick. "There are no survivors? No prisoners? We somehow killed *all* of them? There were over three hundred!"

"Three-hundred-seventy-one, to be exact," Fitzpatrick replied, already familiar with the report from the Shanghai office. "And we didn't kill them, certainly not all of them. They estimate only two hundred or so died from actual combat wounds. Several others had only minor injuries; a few had no injuries at all. But all of those appear to have died from poisoning, and the only explanation is that it was self-administered."

The Regent dropped the tablet and it clattered on the tabletop, "You're telling me one-hundred-fifty people committed suicide? Why? To avoid capture? What did they think we would do to them?"

"Identify them. Perhaps even interrogate them. Both are reasonable expectations," the admiral opined. "I understand it is a common tactic in resistance or terrorist cells; it's a way to avoid revealing other conspirators. But I've never heard of a case of this magnitude."

The Regent pressed his hands to his forehead and leaned back in his chair. "My God. Is that what we've become? Are we the Nazis? We now have an armed underground resistance trying to drive out our occupation force!"

Fitzpatrick shook her head, "Sir, that's not it. This wasn't some improvised group of noble freedom fighters using an odd collection of obsolete weapons and homemade explosives." She took the tablet and selected a different page, thrusting it towards the Regent. "This was a large, highly trained force with advanced weapons. We found two examples of railguns and wreckage from several more. This action was taken by a government – the People's Republic of China."

"And you can prove this?" the Regent demanded.

Fitzpatrick pointed to the tablet, "The railguns are among the most advanced weapons on the planet; you can't order these things online.

Their other weapons and the aircraft are the latest models used by the People's Liberation Army. But none of them have any identifying marks. Someone had to convince multiple factories to produce these untraceable items." She leaned back in her seat, "We are using DNA tracing to identify the deceased. So far, every one of the people we can match has some connection to the PLA. The most intriguing is this one," she swiped a few pages on the tablet to display a military personnel record. "Major Ping Youxia. Until two years ago, he was a senior member of their Oriental Sword specials ops team. Then he simply disappears from the system; no mention of his new assignment."

The Regent studied the record, ignoring the English translation and focusing on the original Chinese text. "What makes him so special?"

Fitzpatrick cleared her throat before answering, "He was the headless body in our captured body armor that they found near the director."

The Regent became very quiet, and Fitzpatrick noticed that his hands were gripping the tablet tighter and tighter. She feared he would snap it in two, but then he relaxed his grip and exhaled. "Well, I can't say I'm sorry with the fate he met. It saves me from ordering the construction of a guillotine." He handed the tablet back to the admiral. "Who do I have to thank for that?"

"Staff Sergeant Heather Mackenzie," Fitzpatrick said with a mix of pride and sorrow. "At least according to Captain Singh. With her last breath, she wrestled Ping's gun away from him and used her sidearm to get under his armor and kill him. By Singh's account, Mackenzie saved Argenta's life."

"I'm sorry I can't thank the sergeant for that," the Regent remarked. "I have to do something for her. Something for all of them; they defended the Commonwealth today. I just never thought that they would have to defend it from our own people."

"They defended you; you were the target," Fitzpatrick reminded him.

"That just means it's my fault. If I never lived in that building, it would never have been attacked," he pointed out.

"And if you never created the Commonwealth, humanity would have been blissfully unaware that the galaxy was planning our extinction. Wondering about 'what might have been' is pointless. We deal with what is!"

Their discussion was interrupted when a steward entered the room to deliver the coffee. Once the crewman left, the Regent walked to the table to retrieve two full mugs. "You're right," he conceded as he placed the mugs on the table. "So how do you suggest we deal with this? They killed three of our soldiers and injured twenty-nine others; who do I punish for that? The perpetrators killed themselves, so I can't punish them. Do I arrest the generals? The president? How do I guarantee this never happens again?" he implored.

Fitzpatrick admitted, "I don't know. That's a decision only you can make. But I will remind you what you always tell me – life doesn't come with guarantees."

The Regent took a long draw from his mug, the warm liquid bringing some comfort. "Maybe I should just borrow a page from Valerius' playbook. Maybe I should rain down destruction from this battle station," the Regent quipped.

"Sir," Fitzpatrick said with exasperation. "I wish you would stop using that term. This is a monitor; it is intended to protect Terra, not attack it. It is not some kind of Deaf Star."

"Death Star," the Regent corrected. "Death Star. Jeez, how can you get *that* wrong?"

Fitzpatrick folded her arms, "Some of us were learning how to fly starships, while others were watching fantasies about them."

"Watch it, Admiral," the Regent chided. "Don't try to give me a history lesson. That movie was twelve years old when you were born. You weren't too busy in school to see it." He shrugged, "Maybe I need to bring back movie night."

"Maybe you're trying to avoid the question," Erin tossed back.

The Regent slapped the table, "You're right. I am." He leaned to his left, "Chika, any luck getting that bastard Wu on the line?"

Nnaji looked up from her work, "No, sir. I checked ten minutes ago; they are still saying the president is unavailable. They do apologize."

"Well, if they apologize, that makes it OK," the Regent commented dryly. "Tell them that if they don't make that little prick *available* in the next thirty minutes, I'm going to erase the Great Wall from their tourist packages." He looked to Fitzpatrick, "Too strong?"

"Just a bit," Erin suggested. "But I'm certain Miss Nnaji will find a more palatable way to get your concerns across."

"Yes," the Regent admitted as he sipped from his mug. "It's a shame really. I would like to see how they react to my actual words."

CHAPTER 15

Terra Monitor East Asia, Terra orbit
2048APR21 06:02 UTC

Coming in just under the deadline, Wu Zhongxun was seated at his usual desk when the display activated in front of the Regent. He was grateful that Nnaji had the forethought to arrange for a set of flags to stand behind him, it gave the impression that the Regent was speaking from his normal seat of power, and not some borrowed bunker in a heavily armed fortress. That would hardly awe the leader of China.

"Regent, I understand you wish to speak. I presume this regards the incident in Shanghai," Wu began, seizing the initiative.

The Regent was almost impressed by the man's audacity. Almost. "That's an interesting term – incident. So clean and antiseptic; no implication of positive or negative motives," the Regent explained. "I was thinking of a more precise term. A coup d'état. A failed coup to be even more precise."

Wu nodded once, "As you prefer. I'm sure you have more information on the nature of the event than I."

The Regent could not believe Wu's reaction to that accusation. The man looked to be completely at ease with all this. "And exactly what information do you have? What have you discovered since our last conversation?"

Wu looked down to a leather folder at his fingertips. Opening it, he peered at the papers within, then looked back up to the Regent, "We have found irregularities in production of certain military equipment, as well as the continuation of research that had been ordered halted by the CMC. There is also evidence of unauthorized movement of personnel to a shuttered facility in Guangxi province. We are still investigating that. But rest assured, we have detained a number of those who appear to be involved. We will learn the truth."

Oh good, the Regent thought, *they've already selected the scapegoats for us. How convenient.* Now he regretted that he did not insist on meeting with Wu in person. He really wanted to beat the arrogant, complacent smile off that man's face. Instead, he would have to beat him with words. "I am surprised you were able to learn so much in such a short time," the Regent began, "Considering how little you knew while this plot was forming for several years." He held up his hand to forestall any retort. "We have also been busy in our investigation." The Regent lifted his own tablet for his review, "Advanced weapons as well as the latest PLA equipment, all without any markings to indicate manufacturer or where or when it was procured. No prisoners. Apparently, these men were under strict orders to avoid capture at any cost." He allowed his face to brighten. "We have been able to identify some of the corpses, though. All appear to have been members of your various special forces units. But I'm sure you have a reasonable explanation for that."

"As I said, Regent, we have detained a number of senior officials connected to unauthorized activities. If there are others, we will discover them. They will all be dealt with. Severely," Wu declared, attempting to resolve the matter on his own terms.

"Yeah … there's a problem, though," the Regent countered. "That's not good enough. I'm not satisfied with just punishing the people you've pre-selected. I want the whole system fixed. The *whole* system." Again, he lifted his tablet, "Effective immediately, I am removing all PLA officers above the rank of captain from duty. They are to vacate their offices and surrender to Security Police by 18:00 local time. They will be held until cleared by Commonwealth Security."

"Regent, this is excessive!" Wu declared.

"Oh, Mister Wu, we are just getting started," the Regent assured his guest, and returned to his list. "At the same time, I am dissolving the current government of the Republic of China. Premier Guo will head up an interim government until new elections can be scheduled."

Wu exploded, "You have no authority to make these demands. The People's Republic of China is a sovereign state. We are not your puppet."

The Regent continued, "About that, we're changing the name. It's just the Republic of China now. I've spoken to the attorney general; she is putting together a working group to review your constitution in order to remove any mention of the Communist Party of China and any provisions or powers assigned to it. I want open elections."

Wu was becoming more agitated by the minute. "You have no power! The people will not stand for this! The Chinese people will decide their fate without alien interference!"

The Regent remained the picture of calm, "That's correct. The people of China will decide. All 1.4 billion of them. Not just the 90 million or so members of your elite. That's what it means to be a republic; to represent the will of the public." The Regent wagged his finger at the display, "You really should study Latin."

Wu pounded the table with his fists. "None of this will happen! None of it! You threaten China? You are nothing! We have defeated all foreigners who thought they could control us. The same will happen to you and your Commonwealth!"

The Regent shook his head slowly, "I'm not threatening China. I'm threating you. *You* are the problem. I want China to be strong and healthy, so I'm removing the cancer before it can do any more damage."

Wu sneered, "You sit on your throne in space. You have no power here." He sat straighter in his chair, "The People's Republic of China formally rejects and withdraws from the Commonwealth. Take your people and go. We have no need for you."

The Regent smiled, "No." He allowed that word to hang in the air for some time. "Do you remember what happened to the president of Russia thirty years ago? Do you remember that little inbred dictator in Korea? What happened to them?" Again, a pause to let the threat sink in. "We removed them. They were a problem, so we removed them. Do you really think I can't do the same thing to you?"

Across the room, Fitzpatrick raised an eyebrow. She was one of only a handful of people who knew just what the Regent was referring to. Thirty years earlier, the Ssenn loaned the Commonwealth teleporters – advanced alien technology that allowed the user to convert matter to energy and then reverse the process at a different location. The Ssenn gave this technology for a specific purpose; it allowed the Commonwealth to eliminate the numerous nuclear stockpiles that existed around the globe at that time. But the Regent found a second use for the teleporters. With it, he was able to kidnap petty tyrants without detection, eliminating them as a threat and at the same time convincing their subordinates to surrender rather than face annihilation on the battlefield.

With this advantage, they were able to establish the Commonwealth with far less bloodshed.

However, the Ssenn removed their teleporters a short while later, satisfied that the Solar Commonwealth would no longer need this power. And that meant the Regent was bluffing now. She just hoped that Wu didn't call that bluff.

Just then, the sound of a door being thrown open caught everyone by surprise. Two soldiers suddenly appeared on either side of the Chinese president. "Wu Zhongxun, you are under arrest," one of the men declared.

"What is this? How dare you!" Wu bellowed, standing. "I am party chairman! Get out!"

"No," a calm voice replied from off-camera. "Please remove this man."

The soldiers grabbed the chairman by his arms, but he refused to go quietly. "Guo! I will have you shot! You little pissant!" The soldiers dragged Wu away from the camera, his threats continued but grew distant as he left the room.

A new figure moved to take the seat recently vacated. "Regent, I trust you will keep your side of our agreement," Guo Shuang stated softly.

"Of course, Premier. I welcome the assistance your interim government provides during this transition. Like you, I have no desire to see Commonwealth troops enforcing these changes if loyal Chinese units are available to do so." The Regent reassured the man. "We will continue to monitor the situation, however."

"We would expect no less," Guo agreed flatly. "Please contact me if you have any concerns." He reached forward and the transmission ended.

Fitzpatrick rose and walked over to the desk, "Well that certainly went better than I could have hoped."

"Yes," the Regent agreed. "Almost too smoothly," he added in thought, then waved away his worries. "We'll just have to keep an eye on them. For now." He checked his band, shaking his head, "I don't know about you, but I could use some rest. It's still a few hours before Argenta wakes up."

Fitzpatrick nodded, "Agreed, sir. I hope you find the accommodations to your liking."

"Are you kidding? Right now, I could sleep on this floor," the Regent tossed back. Clapping his hands, he shooed his assistant. "Run along Chika. Finally, some rest for the weary."

Commonwealth Office (level 0/ground), Shanghai, China
2048APR27 10:10 CST (2048APR27 02:10 UTC)

LT Chu walked through the lobby, still amazed at how quickly the staff had repaired all the evidence of the battle fought here just a week before. All except one wall opposite the entrance doors; this was draped by a heavy tarp. Chu knew what was planned for that section – a memorial wall with three gold and twenty-nine silver stars to recognize the sacrifices of those who defended the building just six days ago. The gold stars were for Mackenzie, Ngaporo and Saman; the silver stars for the injured Guard, Base and Security personnel now recuperating. A pit formed in her stomach when she pictured those men and women and recalled where she was at the time.

Halfway to the lifts, she noticed a familiar face she had not seen since before that fateful day. "Good morning, Lieutenant," Chu remarked as Krejci joined her in front of the lift doors. As always, her simple dark grey suit made her stand out among all the uniformed personnel in the office.

"It's captain now, Lieutenant Chu," Libusa Krejci corrected her colleague. "I'm the new Agent-in-Charge," she beamed.

"Congratulations," Chu returned with enthusiasm, then lowered her voice, "How is Captain Singh?"

Krejci matched the Sentry's volume, "They couldn't save the leg. He's an assistant commander now; in the counterintelligence division." She shrugged, "A desk job. But at least they didn't force him into retirement."

The doors opened with a ping and the two women entered the lift. As the doors closed, Krejci probed, "What about you? Will you be sporting two disks soon?" Her eyes focused on the single disk and ring lieutenant's insignia Chu wore on her uniform collar.

Chu shook her head, "Captain Bruttius isn't going anywhere at the moment." She looked down at her boots, "And it wouldn't feel right abandoning the platoon. Not after failing them when they needed me most."

"You didn't fail them," Krejci said in retort. "We go where we're told and deal with the situation as we find it." She hoped Chu would find something in those words. "I was sorry to hear about Sergeant Mackenzie. She was a hell of a Guardian."

"None finer," Chu agreed readily. "Without her as my platoon sergeant, I'd have washed out years ago."

The doors parted and Chu stepped off, while the new agent-in-charge remained in the lift. "I'm going to twenty-nine. I want to check on the work up there," Krejci informed Chu. "If you're free, how about lunch?"

"Sounds good," I'll meet you in the lobby at noon," Chu answered, then stood back as the doors closed. Turning, she noticed again the state of the corridor. Unlike the lobby, level fourteen still had numerous signs of the firefight that happened here. As with each other time, she shuddered slightly in her anger towards those who attacked her people. *A quick death was too good for them.*

Entering the operations room, she found it still incomplete, but with several additional stations restored since her last visit. "Lieutenant," a man called to get her attention.

"Commander," Chu replied, surprised to find Hirsch on duty. "I thought Lieutenant Hale would be here by now."

Hirsch smiled. "I gave him a few days leave. He'll be back by Friday." He motioned for Chu to join him. "Can you believe that he's never been to the real Chicago. I thought it was time to rectify that oversight."

"Very kind of you," Chu noted. "But aren't you also due some leave time?"

Hirsch looked around the room, he lowered his voice. "If it's all the same, I'd rather not step outside the office grounds until the Regent is done with his reforms. I've spent all the time I care to spend in a PAP detention cell."

"Yes," Chu agreed, "I was lucky to avoid that." She looked to change the subject, "How is Ensign Barzini? Is she back yet?" The more severely injured were evacuated to the Terra Station medical center.

Hirsch hesitated. "She's spending some time with her family in Torino," he admitted, then after a pause confided, "I'm not sure she is coming back."

"I understand," Chu responded. "For what it's worth, my people said she did a fine job. They'd be proud to serve with her again."

"Yes," Hirsch agreed, "so they tell me." His voice drifted off, and there was an awkward silence between the two people who were not here on that fateful day. "So, how can I help you, Ms. Chu?"

She paused before responding, "Well, this might be a little awkward. Captain Bruttius is downstairs arguing with the local authorities about expanding the landing area. He also wants it permanently secured from the public. He was hoping the duty Base officer would join him and make it an official request, since your service is in operational command."

Hirsch stared at Chu for a long count. "All right. But if I end up in a Chinese prison, I'm going to make sure you get the cell right next to me."

"I understand, sir," Chu agreed.

Hirsch nodded, then moved towards the door, "Come along, Lieutenant. Time to face the dragon."

Terra Station, Terra orbit
2048APR29 10:35 UTC

The Regent watched from the couch as Argenta slowly glided around the room, inspecting items and making notes in her tablet. The mobile chair she sat in brought back memories of a similar conveyance he was required to use when they first met, so many years earlier. The irony was not lost on either of them.

"Do you have to do this now?" he asked.

"*Saint Lawrence* arrives tonight and is departing on the first at noon. When do you suggest I do this?" she returned, still making notes.

"I know when the courier is scheduled. But you'll miss Commonwealth Day," he declared.

Placing her stylus on the tablet's face, she looked up. "You do know that they celebrate in Nova Roma, don't you? I should arrive in time to witness the festivities. Unless *someone* interferes with the departure," she looked at him sternly.

The Regent was growing frustrated; she had an answer for all his complaints. "But you're taking everything," he whined.

Quintilius looked at her partner oddly, "Over thirty years, I have acquired a number of items. But trust me, not a tenth of the junk you have procured. Believe me, there is far more that will remain here than will travel with me."

"Yes," the Regent admitted, "but why do you have to take all of it? All of your things?"

Argenta slapped the arm of her chair, "Because I do not know when I will return." She wavered for a moment, trying to catch her breath.

"Are you alright?" he pleaded from the couch. The past few days, he had made it a point to always be seated in Argenta's presence, hoping to minimize any strain on her neck or back if she had to look up at him. But now, he wanted to rush to her side.

Quintilius raised a hand, preventing his action, "I will be fine, if you stop arguing. You were warned about this by Doctor Nonius."

He looked down chastened. "I know. I just thought you paid her to say that."

Argenta smiled slightly. "Then you are finally showing wisdom. I would have done just that, but in this case, it was the doctor who made the suggestion. So please honor her wishes. And mine."

"I still don't see why you can't recuperate here," he complained.

"Because our doctor recommended it," she reminded him. "I have made arrangements for an estate outside the city, near the coast. Nonius believes the climate there will be to my benefit."

"It won't be safe. You're bound to run into supporters of Valerius, even after all these years." The Regent was grasping for any leverage to change her mind.

Argenta scoffed, "You still don't know us. Valerius never had any hold on the public; his support was based solely on his promises for reunion. Once that was achieved, we Romans had no need for him and his plottings. Indeed, since you are the one who actually made reunion possible, there are no kind words these days for his time as Consul." While Quintilius was told by her doctor not to argue, no one could stop her from delivering a lecture. "True Romans have no need for would-be emperors. Present company excluded, of course."

The Regent smiled briefly at the gibe. "Then I'll go with you. I can do my job anywhere. I just proved that last week."

"No," Argenta ruled. "You are the leader of the Commonwealth. The *Solar* Commonwealth. Sol is here and here is where you must remain." She raised her arms weakly to shoulder height. "This is your capital. Here on this station."

"Some capital," he muttered. "No marble buildings. No grand parks. No statues. And now I can't return to one of the main cities on the planet. Which means I probably can't go back to New York either."

Quintilius nodded, "True. You cannot be seen to grant favor to one of the old powers. Not now, at least."

The Regent sighed, "So I must stay, and you must go."

"I'm sorry," she replied. "We both knew this day would come. I wish it were not now, but I do not control the fates. I am old and now I am weak; when I die, I wish it to be in my homeland. Not in some container floating over a world that was never my home."

The Regent struggled to hold his emotions down. He knew she was right, and he hated himself for making her say what they both knew to be true. Instead, he tried to adopt a brave face, nodding, "But I can still visit you. Right?"

Argenta nodded slowly, "I will allow one visit per year. Per *Terranian* year," she amended, granting herself a little more time between visits. "Call first, though. Now that I will be free of your Christian morality, I plan to take a lover." She added a smirk; they both knew it was a lie.

"Well, I do not," the Regent answered solemnly. "I can never replace you, Argenta."

"Be careful, Regent," she advised him. "You will live long after I am gone. Several hundred years. Do not make promised you cannot keep." She maneuvered her chair closer, "Or I will need to remind you when we meet again in the afterlife."

"Promise?" he asked, inching closer to her.

"I recall a threat to bed some Tyndaline princess several years ago," she countered as their lips drew closer, finally brushing softly. They held that position for several seconds, until the Regent eased back onto the couch.

"Oooh, I forgot all about that. I need to make some calls," he teased. He slid past her and walked towards the bedroom. "Coming?"

ACKNOWLEDGEMENTS

After four books covering humanity's interaction with aliens, this is the first story of the Solar Commonwealth to feature only humans. While meeting aliens is always interesting, sometimes it is important to understand ourselves. Too often, science fiction presents an idealized utopian future where a unified human race is in conflict with the galaxy. I think the journey to that unity, with all the bumps and detours, is just as important to explore.

For the first time, most of the action takes place on Earth, in a real city, even if I did insist on creating a fictional building. There are no great space battles, with only a few scenes taking place on orbital stations circling the planet.

And it's a chance to see the Regent deal with his unique situation, watching people struggle to protect a future they will never see, but he will.

Once again, I thank my wife, Kate, for serving as my proofreader and editor. Without her, none of this would happen. And more importantly, most of it would be gibberish.

My children, James and Erin, continue to review my work, pointing out my mistakes and making sure I don't accidently contradict the future I already covered in earlier works.

I want to thank Jan Kennedy for her continued interest and for acting as my one-woman international promotion department, carrying the Commonwealth around the globe, one trip at a time.

Finally, I again thank all those who have written reviews of the previous books. There is nothing better than seeing when something you created is enjoyed by another. I hope that after reading this episode of the Regent's saga, you will take the time to drop a note with your thoughts – good, bad or other. All are welcome.

MAIN CHARACTERS

Terrans

Solar Commonwealth:

Regent – Prime Executive; head of state of the Solar Commonwealth.

Argenta Quintilius – former Executive Director of the Solar Commonwealth.

Jiang Weijia – Director of Defense.

Solar Fleet:

Erin Caitlin Fitzpatrick (PhaPadraic) – Vice Admiral; Chief of Fleet Operations.

Caoimhin Cinnéidigh – Captain, commanding officer, light cruiser *Bavaria*.

Solar Base:

Albrecht Hirsch – Lieutenant Commander; commanding officer, SCO Shanghai.

Jonathan Hale – Lieutenant (junior grade); operations officer, SCO Shanghai.

Monica Barzini – Ensign; security officer, SCO Shanghai.

Solar Guard:

Attalus Bruttius – Captain; senior platoon leader, 4th Platoon, Company A, 3rd Sentry Battalion.

Chu Daxia – Lieutenant; platoon leader, 3rd Platoon, Company A, 3rd Sentry Battalion.

Heather Mackenzie – Staff Sergeant; platoon sergeant, 3rd Platoon, Company A, 3rd Sentry Battalion.

Solar Flight:

Janella Concepcion – Sublieutenant; pilot, Red Falcon 4, 12th Interceptor Squadron.

Commonwealth Security:

Ranbir Singh – Captain; agent-in-charge, Regent's protective detail.

People's Republic of China:

Wu Zhongxun – President; head of state.

People's Liberation Army:

Sun Qiliang – Colonel; head of Department 828.

Ping Youxia – Major; commanding officer, Black Tiger team.

Xu – Captain; deputy commander, Black Tiger team.

Ma – First Lieutenant; combat engineering officer, Black Tiger team.

Liang – First Lieutenant; platoon leader, Black Tiger team.

People's Armed Police:

Yang Xiwang – Captain; commanding officer, Company 7, 1st Mobile Detachment, Shanghai.

United States of America:

Lucian Scott-Marshall – President; head of state.

GLOSSARY

laowai – Chinese. Informal term for non-Asian foreigners; sometimes used as a pejorative.

wo bu mingbai – Chinese. "I don't understand."

wuxing hongqi – Chinese. "Five Star Red Flag." Common term for the national flag of the People's Republic of China.

ABOUT THE AUTHOR

John Lallier is a veteran of the software industry with a lifelong passion for science fiction. After years of toiling away in the back rooms of software companies like a digital elf, he now spends his days sitting in front of a very similar computer creating an imaginary universe with dozens of worlds and races. And now he can only blame himself for the terrible coffee. At least the view out of the window is nicer.

You are all invited to pull up a chair and bring your own mug of coffee or tea (Earl Grey, hot of course), and tour the worlds of the Commonwealth. If you find yourself enjoying the journey, you can find more at www.jclpress.com.

John lives in New York with his wife, two children and their cats. He's relatively certain the cats are plotting to take over the universe. So he's brought in a new puppy to help even the odds. More on that in Book 5.